Autumn's Ballad

"An enchanted love written in the leaves"

A Novelette In Verse By:
C. L. Pinto Martinez

Illustrations & Photography By:
C. L. Pinto Martinez

Published by: *House of Chay*
An imprint of: *Hey Chay Press* in conjunction with
Hadassah's Crown Publishing, LLC
634 NE Main St #1263
Simpsonville, SC 29681
Website: hadassahscrownpublishing.com

6x9 Paperback Edition ISBN: 979-8-9991199-8-8

Printed in the United States

To the person I never was
To the person I always wanted to be
To the person I detested the most
To the person I always hoped to become
To the person I never thought I was ever good enough for
To the person I eventually was proud to become
Thank you for putting up with me all these years
Thank you for loving me
Thank you for showing me how to love you
Thank you for patiently waiting until I finally did.

Autumn's Ballad is a poignant novelette that explores the profound themes of life, change, and legacy through the lens of Autumn. Weaving together poetry, short stories, illustrations, and photography, it offers a reflective exploration of how the changing seasons mirror the cycles of life and the enduring impact of relationships.

At its core, *Autumn's Ballad* delves into the protagonist's contemplation of legacy — what they hope to leave behind, and the tension between regret and acceptance. This internal struggle highlights the journey of reconciling what has been lost with the richness of experiences gained. The narrative emphasizes the importance of connection, illustrating how relationships shape our identities and influence our sense of purpose. Ultimately, it underscores the transformative power of change and the enduring bonds that guide us through life's journey.

The book is thoughtfully structured, with poems presented as "Vignettes," short stories as "Chronicles," and illustrations and photographs as "Ekphrasis." This intentional format enhances the reader's experience, clearly distinguishing each form and adding depth to the overall narrative.

Contents

Introduction

Greetings, dear traveler, seeker of secrets and whispers in the wind. Welcome to the threshold of a world where shadows dance, a tapestry of golden hues and flowing leaves await your arrival, and the air is thick with stories of legacies, genealogies, and histories rooted deep within the sacred earth. This is a realm where the spirit of Autumn reveals a hidden garden that awakens only during the seasonal shifts, echoing the wisdom of our ancestors, the Indigenous peoples who revered the land and its cycles.

I'm Lyra, a flicker of moonlight guiding you through the veils of dusk. As the seasons shift and the vibrant hues of fall embrace the landscape, I walk alongside you, illuminating the paths of those entwined in this intricate dance of life. Each character you meet embodies a fragment of existence — some radiate the warmth of fleeting sunlight, while others conceal the shadows of regret. My purpose is to unveil the layers beneath their journeys, revealing the rich lessons hidden within.

In each chronicle, you will discover a beginning and an end, reflecting the essence, purpose, and challenges that accompany you on your journey with Autumn. As you delve deeper, you will encounter the spirit of change, where the tempestuous challenges presented by Rowan, whose name whispers of resilience, intersect with the comforting embrace of Maple, a symbol of nurturing and growth.

Together, we will explore profound themes of life, change, and legacy through the lens of this enchanting season. The narrative unfolds as an emotional journey, centering on the protagonist's reflections on the legacy they hope to leave behind. This exploration evokes a tension between regret and acceptance, echoing the stories passed down through generations of Indigenous cultures. It highlights the struggle to reconcile what has been lost with the richness of experiences gained over time, inviting you to reflect on the enduring connections that shape our identities.

Through these poetic explorations, we will emphasize the significance of connection, illustrating how relationships shape our identities and influence our understanding of self and purpose. The story weaves together themes of enduring bonds and the transformative effects of change, reflecting the teachings of Indigenous cultures that remind us of our place within the larger web of life.

Together, you and I will embark on a journey along a carefully woven path that invites an air of mystery and intrigue. The poetic glimpses are called "Vignette," a term that encapsulates fleeting moments and snapshots of emotion, inviting you to pause and savor the beauty hidden within brief yet profound experiences. "Chronicles" unfold as rich narratives, akin to a historical tapestry that intertwines the lives of characters, revealing their individual and collective stories as they evolve over time. Finally, the striking imagery, designs, and photography are celebrated as "Ekphrasis," a term that pays homage to the art of visual storytelling, allowing you to immerse yourself in scenes that transcend the confines of language. This imaginative arrangement enhances your navigation through the narrative, illuminating the unique qualities of each form while unveiling the deeper connections that bind them together.

So, take my hand as we delve deeper into this enchanting chronicle. Together, we will explore the delicate balance of light and dark, joy and sorrow, and the timeless dance of life unfolding with every breath of wind. Allow the mysteries of these characters to resonate within you as we illuminate their stories and embrace the transformative power of change.

Welcome to the chronicles of Autumn—welcome to the world through my eyes. As you settle into this collection of poems, short stories, and photography, let the warmth of a cozy fire wrap around you. With a cup of spicy hot chai tea in hand, may each word draw you in, inviting you to reflect, to feel, and to fall in love with the season's magic time and again.

Signed,
Lyra

Autumn's Best Friend

Prologue

The Season of Change

What speaks to change more than the season and the passing of time? As we carefully tread the beveled passageways through forests and everglades, we encounter travelers and passerby's—some whose stays are brief, others whose encounters are lengthy. Each on a journey to be captivated by the elegance, resistance, resilience, and simple permanence of Autumn's embrace.

Listen to Lyra, as I weave a tale never told, a story worth sharing, its weight in gold.

We begin at the beginning, with Alder's birth—a story so heartwarming it could melt the earth. The announcement springs thoughts full of wonder and hope, ushering in an age of promise and innocence. Alder, unaware of the burdens that lie ahead, is filled with the joy of new life. A pure celebration. A protector of all that is innocent. Alder's presence is a gentle reminder of what it means to begin anew, to embrace the world with untainted eyes and a heart full of possibility.

Along the way, we meet others on the trail—each one intricately woven into the fabric of Autumn's tale. Gale, the embodiment of chaos, and Cyrus, the harbinger of unspoken tensions, each play their part in shaping Autumn's journey. They stir the air, shifting the course of events, and introduce both obstacles and lessons that Autumn must face. With every breath of wind, they remind Autumn that the road is never linear—change is constant, unpredictable, and often difficult.

Next, we meet Crystal and Lark—beacons of clarity and freedom in Autumn's path. Crystal, a steady force of wisdom, helps Autumn navigate the complexities of identity, providing clarity in times of confusion. Lark, full of exuberance and adventure, encourages Autumn to embrace the unknown, reminding her that change is not something to fear but something to be celebrated. These two stand as symbols of self-discovery and growth, urging Autumn to find her place in the ever-shifting world around her.

Yet, not all figures on this journey are so easily understood. The rebellion and tension of a tender age bring Willow and Drake into the spotlight. Willow, full of envy and longing, reflects the internal strife that plagues Autumn in her adolescence. A mirror of Autumn's own struggles with self-acceptance, Willow's jealousy sparks moments of introspection and self-doubt, forcing Autumn to question who she is and what she truly values. Drake, on the other hand, embodies the restless spirit of youth—impulsive, wild, and unpredictable. His influence challenges Autumn to step outside of her comfort zone, teaching her the consequences of action and inaction alike.

Then, there is Riley—ever cynical, his perspective on the world shaped by disappointment and loss. He tests Autumn's idealism, challenging her to confront the harsh realities of life. His doubts push Autumn to confront her own beliefs and question her understanding of truth and purpose. In contrast, Skye offers wisdom—gently reminding Autumn that change, though often difficult, is an inevitable part of the human experience. Skye's quiet grace reflects the beauty of acceptance and peace, teaching Autumn that wisdom comes not from avoiding hardship but from embracing it.

Briar embodies resilience — an unwavering force through the seasons of Autumn's life. Briar's lessons come in moments of crisis, when Autumn's spirit feels fragile and the weight of the world is too much to bear. Briar's presence reminds Autumn that strength is found not in avoiding struggle, but in rising from it time and time again. Through Briar, Autumn learns the profound power of resilience — an inner fortitude that allows one to keep going even when the way ahead is unclear.

And then, there is Fern — nurturing, comforting, and deeply connected to the pulse of life. Fern reminds Autumn of the importance of community and relationships — the ties that bind us together through change, loss, and growth. It is through Fern that Autumn learns that no journey is ever truly solitary. The bonds we form along the way, the love we give and receive, shape the very core of who we are. In Fern, Autumn finds not only a reminder of the beauty of connection but also a deep understanding of its necessity.

Each one of these figures — Gale, Cyrus, Crystal, Lark, Willow, Drake, Riley, Skye, Briar, and Fern — leaves an imprint, shaping Autumn's journey in subtle yet profound ways. Together, they create a tapestry of experiences that mark Autumn's growth — moments of joy, sorrow, rebellion, wisdom, and love. Each individual plays a role in helping Autumn understand the complexities of her own existence. From innocence to maturity, from simplicity to depth, the lessons of these figures will carry Autumn through the ebbs and flows of life.

Lyra has seen it all. Standing far above the earth, casting light upon the world below, Lyra has observed the unfolding of Autumn's story. Silent, yet constant, Lyra has been the ever-present witness to the beauty and struggles of life. With a heart that knows both the weight of time and the lightness of existence, Lyra has quietly watched as Autumn's journey has shaped the world around her. Lyra is more than just a narrator—she is the embodiment of time itself, carrying the wisdom of the seasons, the wisdom of change.

Autumn's Ballad is more than a melody—it is a symphony in harmony, sung by every living thing. It is the sound of life, growth, loss, and renewal. It represents every change that no other season can sing, every whisper of the wind, every rustle of the leaves, and every beat of the heart. *Autumn's Ballad* is the song of the earth itself, played through the creatures of the land, sea, and sky, and resonating in the hearts of humanity.

We are simply guests in the audience of this mighty great hall, witnessing a performance that has been ongoing since time began. In this concert, every life has its part to play, and every note sung contributes to the grand symphony of existence. Let me be your guide, your conductor, as we embark on the greatest show of all—the beautiful, transformative, and ever-changing season of Autumn, better known as Fall.

Chronicle 1

Alder: The Dawn of Life

The green grassy knoll has taken its final bow, and the rays of sunshine now paint the summer sky, filling it with glorious shades of red, orange, and yellow. Trees begin shedding their summer skins, ushering in a new dawn, eagerly anticipating the arrival of something new. The earth transforms, crafting a patchwork quilt that mirrors Grandma's—each square representing our place in it. Bespoke, woodsmoke, everglades, chimney smoke. The forest stirs, and it has spoken: Welcome, one and all, to the greatest season the land has ever known—Autumn, also known as Fall. Summer departs, leaves dance to the ground, waving farewell, while birds chirp their final curtain call.

Pumpkin and cinnamon fill the air, once thick with the sultry heat of summer, now cooling with the scents of apple, maple, and nutmeg on repeat. The metallic aromas of orange marmalade blend with peach cobbler and tulips, mingling with the last grass clippings before the seasons change. Early morning dew gives way to mist and fog—the presence of Autumn is felt, both near and far.

Can you imagine never knowing the purest warmth of the sun? The gentle embrace of a lover by a roaring fire, on a bed of wildflowers beneath a star-filled sky. The softness of the horizon welcomes you, dipping low to offer an audience. The evening sky reflects a peloton palette of my wildest imagination—a dance of colors gentler than a single drop of water streaming from the fountain of everlasting life from on high.

Light rises before us, bathed in the golden rays of summer's sun. Clouds, soft as cotton, plump as marshmallows, pure as driven snow. Amber hues awaken, bringing scents of caramel and chocolate, combined with melodies of melancholy and fragments of mixology—from chai spice to arabica chili beans—it all means everything to me. The days soften and grow shorter. Time dwindles, and the sense of urgency approaches. Now tinged with evening shadows—deep ambrosia, amber rose. Ebony, ivory, uniquely qualified, stretching long into the evening tide.

A new day has dawned, and with it, the golden gaze of the sun spreads its light across the land. It's a time when forest creatures begin their preparations, and humans start to reap the fruits of what they've sown. Months of waiting—waiting for things to ripen, take root, and mature—have led to this moment. Row by row, line by line, precept by precept, the earth weaves it all together.

There is an age of innocence we call adolescence, the age of immaturity and boundless curiosity. It is a time when we are free to imagine the impossible, unrestrained by ingenuity. In this spirit, we rise to give hope a jolt, to expand and grow—a vital force for change. As the season shifts, the sands of time wind down. A new day arrives, and the town fills with people, eager to begin the long-awaited rituals of fall. Together, they welcome Alder, the destined arrival of Autumn. Alder, a cherished addition to the family, a gift to be celebrated.

The birds will sing of its arrival, and the trees will sway in joyous harmony. All creatures—of land, sea, and sky—unite in allegiance to this new arrival, the apple of Autumn's eye. Let's take a deep dive into the hot springs, Earth's Olympic-sized pool. Cleanse off the past, stepping into the new. Fancy robes, evening attire. Delicious delicacies and apple cider. Herbal teas, if you please. Trumpets, clarinets—an orchestral symphony worthy of the highest praise, refined elegance, reminiscent of royalty. A dance, a party, a soiree indeed. Can we dance, shout, and sing with glee? Alder, my sweet baby, has finally come to be.

The world exhales. The time we've been waiting for has arrived. Filled with wonder and oozing with pride, joy fills this moment, the most precious time we've known. Alder, a chosen vessel for tomorrow's hope. We all experience that "aha" moment when everything suddenly becomes clear—and here, it is no different. Autumn has come to recognize that time waits for no one—not even something as grand as it.

Brushstrokes of navies and taupe, flakes of copper, silver, and gold, hues of bronze, topped by a utopia of evening jade. Who can dare to question nature's profound ways? My heart is full, filled with gladness. Free from sin, humanity's madness. Ease of life, immense intensity of simple plea-sures—waterfalls and hiking trails, evening strolls and windmills, scents of rosemary, thyme, and chirata leaves—all pleasing to the essence of sensitivity.

The power of love, hope, joy, and peace resides within us all, and Alder will be the symbol that unites us. It is the tapestry that connects us all, the greatest gift of all. Cheers to new life, new birth, and new beginnings. Salud to everlasting affection, to the communication that transcends, and to the eternal appreciation of what this symbol truly means: unity.

Ekphrasis 1:

Sonnets of the Season

Hey chay
Ekphrasis 1:
Sonnets of
the Season

Chronicle 2

Gale: The Winds of Chaos

The makings of a perfect storm—wind, heat, followed by rain—are reminiscent of love, life, and pain. Each element dances together like the ebb and flow of human emotion: fierce winds of change stir the heart, and heat from passion or anger fuels the chaos that envelops the soul. Yet, even within this tumult, there is a promise of renewal, of new life rising from the aftermath. From the winds of change, life's storms are born, offering us both moments of hardship and growth. In the whirlwind, we may feel lost, but in the heart of it all, there is also beauty, an alluring chaos that speaks its own name: Gale.

The silent echo of a storm's roar is like envy whispered in the night—sharp, unrelenting, yet somehow a call to action. The trees bend, the forest animals scramble, all staking their claim in the struggle for survival, for meaning, for identity in this ever-changing world. Life is messy, unpredictable—like the complex fusion of sweet and savory, salty caramel and spicy pecan, or the stale perfume that lingers too long, the mingling of contradictions in our hearts.

Aroma swirls through the air, laced with both the desire for change and the weight of the past. Distant sounds punctuate the scene: the grinding of metal on metal, the clash of emotions, like bronze armories scraping against one another, worn by time and battle. These sounds echo with the knowledge that every challenge we face, like a cemetery plot, marks the end of one journey and the birth of another.

And yet, this birth is never without pain. The rude awakening of a storm's arrival is sharp and jarring, like the drip drop of rain or the clickety clack of destiny's approach, carrying with it the promise of thunderbolts of transformation, like the unexpected joy found in the most chaotic of moments.

And as the storm subsides, we see the traces left behind: the delicate paths of deer tracks, leading us forward. Even in the storm's wake, there is a sense of clarity, a reawakening, a reminder that after the fiercest tempests come the moments of peace, where life, reborn anew, promises joy. In the chaos, there is always a chance for growth, for meaning, for birth. The storm has passed, and with it, so too has the pain, leaving behind the seeds of joy ready to bloom in the heart of a world forever changed.

Ekphrasis 2:

Cascade of Autumn Dreams

Ekphrasis 2:
Cascade of
Autumn Dreams

Ekphrasis 3:

Echoes Beneath the Fall

Ekphrasis 3:
Echoes Beneath
the Falls

Vignette 1

The Essence of Beginnings

Autumn Is My Name

I am blessed beyond measure. Filled with all the love,
peace, and joy promised me
I am worthy of all greatness and grace that is bestowed
upon me
I am filled with life, energy, and dare I say harmony
To know me is to truly behold beauty
Autumn is my name, for I am she

I am dependent upon nothing, yet all depend on me
To feed and clothe them, to provide shelter, strength, and
even a pharmacy
My herbs and fruits will carry you through
When winter comes along to bury you
To know me is to truly realize my value
Autumn is my name, for I am she

Take a stroll in my forest and hear the sounds of laughter
As parents and children play and make memories to carry
on even after
They see my colors fade away slightly
The winds and the rains bid farewell ever so politely
To know me is to witness the end of the very best side of
me
Autumn is my name, for I am she

I have risen high above all circumstances that surround me
I have overcome every challenge that has been thrown
before me
I have cast aside all the care for tomorrow
For tomorrow is only filled with sorrow
To know me is to truly see my whimsical identity

Autumn is my name, for I am she
I am beauty personified
I am light glorified
I am love magnified
I am wisdom amplified
To know me is to recognize all of my armory
Autumn is my name, for I am she

People of the First Light

My aboriginal children from all around the globe, hear my call, I honor you as you honor me. Our relationship runs deeper than the ocean and higher than the tallest mountain peaks.

My primordial babies, birth in the natural cycles of the sun, light, and land, I beseech thee to stand and reclaim your rightful place as rulers and masters of this world. Your legacy is not one of defeat but of greatness, not of despair but endless hope, not of hate but of unwavering love.
At the very first light of dawn, it was you who were born.

Sacred, transformative, at a time when the world shifts from darkness
to light, all will gather again to behold your marvelous sight. A spiritual heritage, boundless connection, your birthright is at your feet, you need only to walk upon it and embrace it.

Uphold your role and hallowed duty to bring light to the world, wisdom to your people, and knowledge to your children. Where the first light emerges from the darkness, you are the sun. When the earth turns cold, from you its inhabitants will feel warm.

Now is your time of enlightenment, the dawning of wisdom, understanding, and a new spiritual path to be undertaken. Take hold your scepter, and be crowned once again, my king, my queen, my chosen flock. My people of the first light.

Autumn's Embrace

In the depths of the arctic where cold overtakes you and shatters the bones, there are times when warmth can be felt by the boldness of the twenty-four-hour son. This is the essence of Autumn's embrace. Breaking the barriers filled by endless nights, comes the rays and blessings of the golden light. Significant for all, far and wide, a beauty to behold, a sacred moment, filled with pride.

The light of Autumn, a softer, golden, and shorter hue, bursts the cunning and dramatic shifts of the Arctic's darkest winter blues. Though Autumn brings with it an end through the fading of warmth in preparation for winter, the extreme conditions of the Arctic's light governed by its polar location, is overtaken by Autumn's dedication.

The Arctic, a place of stark contrasts and extreme cold, still plays a vital role. Yet Autumn is a temperate season marked by warmth destined to give way to the coolness of the winter season. This is the way of nature, displaying vibrant color changes one last time before the onset of winter, is the only reason.

No longer muted, icy, and ethereal, Autumn brings with it warm, vibrant hues before the landscape becomes bare for winter. With the stillness of winter in the Arctic, the inhabitants are forced underground or to flee, but it is Autumn's embrace that beckons thee.

Dance of the Chickadees

Piano keys play the melody of the wind sweeping beneath
our wings
Sounds of the clarinet fluttering sweet whispers in our ears
This it began, this sweet song we sang, as we stroll and hop
along the tree tops
Moonlight glistens, precious kisses, whimsical wishes,
blissful beginnings

Say you will stay with me forever, yet forever's not enough
The road will be bumpy, this life will Be tough
The waves will be harsh and the winds will be rough
There is no love like ours in heaven or on earth

Dance my sweet little chickadee and show me how much you
dare to care
Midnight is coming sooner than expected, a storm is on the
horizon
Winter is yet still far away, Autumn's love birds will fall,
will fail,
Nothing is forever, no two creatures, nor two things, nor
those of past, present, or future

Dance with me my precious chickadee as we make our love
plain for all to see
Your hand in mine, let's make only sweet memories,
convey our love eternally
Your head next to mine, no pillow can compare, your arm
in mine, loving and fair
Your embrace is as a warm cup of sider on a cold Autumn
day, a breath of fresh air

Darkness falls, nature calls, separation is inevitable too

No two creatures, no two things, nor those of past, present,
or future will ever last
Sing and dance as you may your so-called romance will
fade away
As the trees lose their leaves, so will many lovers be, alone
to suffer with only a memory of a single melody

Nay, say the lovers, as they dance to their heart's content,
no other dare contend
Tears of joy stream down their face, love is promised to
those who endure until the end
As if on repeat, their dance continues, not missing a beat,
no missteps ever saw, their love knew no flaw, yet
continued to soar and climb
The dance of the chickadees lasts for a lifetime, no wonder
they are declared as Autumn's most treasured lovers of all
time

The Miracle of Motherhood

Autumn is a season that can be cold to the touch,
The bone crushing breeze can sometimes be too much,
A flickering light would bring forth fresh air,
A symbol of hope, escape from despair.

In a world where mothers are expected,
I stood, unseen, in the shadows,
Always blending into the background,
Where voices drowned the silent heart.

I dreamed of freedom,
The wind of Autumn sweeping through my hair,
Escaping the mundane life that others danced to,
I simply prayed for a life that was uniquely mine.

But life, nature, perhaps even god, it seems, has its own
design —
As the leaves wither away, so too did my
Plans unravel right before my eyes
As the heart learns to bend, and the trees vow never to
break
A moment of joy arose from the heartbreak

In a moment, joy and fear entwined,
A miracle whispered: "soon you will be mine."
Shocked by the news, I sought the truth,
Persistently, frantically, almost irrationally I scattered

Scoring across multiple hospital rooms
Two, three opinions echoed back the same —
Pregnant, at twenty, in chaos I spun,
The dreams of my youth suddenly undone.

Forsaken, forgotten, I felt the weight,
Yet in darkness, a flicker ignited the soul,
That feeling of lost became a fierce flame,
As I grasped the love that would rewrite my role.

Autumn has taken so much from me
I paced and thought to myself frantically
Is this the coming-of-age story of my destiny
Is this who I was preordained to be

It mattered not, for soon my life would not be my own
My daughter is set to arrive soon
My light, my love, the stars, and the moon
Yet trouble was foretold, and warnings were bold

Autumn never lost a fight, never waned in the night
Physicians with all their fancy medical degrees
Never took the time to truly see, me
A feeling a dread swept the room,
Good thing I have a broom

Doctors warned, "She may not survive."
I refused to believe, I knew she would thrive
Suddenly in that labor, a voice rose within —
"No, she will live, for I know my God!"

With each contraction, my spirit soared,
I prayed for her life, surrounded by light,
A circle of faith, by the men of old
hands joined in trust, we beseech God's grace

Born a miracle, tiny yet bold,
One pound, five ounces — a story unfolds,
The odds stacked high, yet hope filled the air,
As prayers were lifted, my heart laid bare.

She taught me the meaning of love profound,
To fight, to cherish, to rise from the ground,
What once felt like burdens became gifts divine,
In her eyes, I found purpose, my life's design.

Autumn, I thought, had taken so much from me
Yet, a gift was given so incredibly
As I embrace my destiny, fierce and free,
No longer afraid of who I could be.

I never knew the beauty and power that Autumn held
Until your hands were in mine, naked and bare
For in loving her, I discovered my worth,
A miracle of motherhood, a new birth.

Sweet September

It was a beautiful day in September,
When the flowers bloomed and the forest creatures
remembered,
How much Autumn is filled with life, and its love is so
tender,
Grateful to be one of its chosen few, family, community
member.

Fruits and veggies go into the blender,
A hangover cure for those on a bender,
Crafting a story of surrender,
My lover, my king, my knight, my defender.

The battlefield—bittersweet, the soldier remembers,
The families away, awaiting the sound of golden timbers.
Horses and wagons, trucks and cars, all the same—
forgotten tenders,
Pillage and loot, riots and wars, all leave the same awful
scars, the fire's ember.

Sweet September is the call of a welcomed sweet surrender,
When all the wounded, lost, and overcome are welcomed
home, our great defender.
Soldiers to some, enemies to others, heroes in their own
right, society's forgotten member.
Raise a glass, shout a toast, silent prayer, a feast and roast,
singing praises, the finale, ender.

Shepherd's Pie

It's harvest time! That means Autumn's famous Shepherd's
Pie!
As the days grow shorter and the temperatures dip,
Autumn's world-class dish will surely make your heart
skip.
A perfect meal to nourish both body and soul,
Hearty veggies, tender meats, and a comforting bowl.

In this season when the harvests start to fade,
No love compares to root vegetables in the shade.
The sweet aroma of carrots, parsnips, and turnips fills the
air,
Autumn's bounty, rich and fair.

Autumn's here, and it's time to feast,
Let's sit down and savor the very best, to say the least.
A dish our bellies have longed for,
A delicacy worth waiting for.

Leftovers? Oh, they're a gift to behold,
The flavors grow richer, the story retold.
From late summer to early fall,
It's a season of abundance, of love, and of all.

Harvest Dreams

The world turns golden, red, and amber,
As leaves drift down, and Autumn grows grander.
The air hums with the scent of decaying leaves,
And the warmth of wood smoke carried on the breeze.

The harvest is in, the final fruits of summer,
Carrots, parsnips, leeks, all ready to lumber.
Potatoes, corn, and beets in their prime,
Tomatoes, cucumbers, rye — harvested just in time.

Oatmeal, cornbread, and apple pie,
Comfort and flavor, as the days go by.
Beauty in nature, wealth fills the air,
Root vegetables and slow-cooked meats, beyond compare.

My heart skips a beat in this season so sweet,
With harvest dreams that never retreat.
In every scent, in every taste,
Autumn's blessings are never misplaced.

Who Is Autumn's Father?

Did you know even Autumn has a father?
Everyone, everything thing, on earth and in the sea
Has a parent they can call their own
Autumn has a father, though he is, to some, unknown

But Autumn has his life and love showered from above
Autumn takes pride in the legacy long built
One of courage, of strength, and fortitude
Never ending, long lasting, eternal gratitude

Who is this father of great mystery
Why don't we see him in Autumn's genealogy
Why can't we meet him on teacher's appreciation night
Why doesn't show up, this isn't Autumn's fight

Why doesn't he give Autumn his last name
For goodness sakes, what's his game
Why must others suffer for his mistakes
Autumn's father is a total flake

But Autumn stood proudly and defended him
While others around only tried to pretend
That their words caused more harm than good
Autumn's father was sorely misunderstood

You see the is a story few others know
Of love lost, pain and suffering tossed here and there
Autumn's father was always around
Even when no one saw him, he could be found

Overlooking Autumn's every step
When Autumn fell, its father wept
Caring for, sharing in, and providing all it would ever need
Autumn was a miracle from which its father breathed

Golden Glow

Imagine it's a late September afternoon,
The sun dips low, the sky begins to swoon.
A hint of coolness stirs the air,
Perfect for picking apples, beyond compare.

At the farmer's market, we spent the day,
Wandering from stall to stall, tasting along the way.
Skipping and laughing, counting our blessings,
A day to remember, with no second guessing.

Gathering at the community story,
Barnyard dances, a celebration of glory.
Fresh vegetables, a meal to share,
Golden apple pie — what a steal, beyond compare.

The day turns longer, warmth gives way to chill,
Returning home, with time to be still.
The scent of garlic, onions, and thyme fills the air,
Mac and cheese, peach cobbler, and cider — comfort so rare.

What's that? Brownies! Chocolate lovers beware,
The oven tempts me, making my belly despair.
Craving the scent, as the pie slowly bakes,
Autumn's magic in every move it makes.

A golden glow, a marmalade breeze,
Pecan pie, fruit bowls, and the quiet of trees.
Outside, the amber leaves begin to fall,
Inside, we savor the season, embracing it all.

The world outside settles into Autumn's rhythm,
While we enjoy a dish that feels like heaven.

Comforting, hearty, flavors of the earth,
Sweet and filling, a season of rebirth.

A golden glow in September's embrace —
A dish that captures Autumn's grace:
Change, abundance, and comfort so deep,
A season to savor, and memories to keep.

Glory Creek

Mystic rivers and elegant forest halls
Hidden behind forces of nature and waterfalls
Witness the first light of fall,
Dancing across the creek, awaiting its curtain call.

Gently the sun touches the earth,
A symbol of wonder, a sign of new birth
My hand stretches out to you
Hoping to touch the essence of morning dew.

Witnesses in real-time, the changing leaves,
Creating a sparkle, an ethereal quality that breathes.
The mist or fog that often lingers in early Autumn
mornings
Adds a hint of mystery, a glimpse of history, a sense of
endless possibility

Life pulses beneath our feet,
A landscape of love, peace, and tranquility, complete.
An otherworldly feeling of romantic beauty,
A sense that we can do anything, boundless and free.

The wind beneath my wings,
The music of my soul, my knees fall weak
The joy the sound brings
This is the marvelous splendor of Glory Creek

Autumn's First Light

Alder witnesses the first light of Autumn, soft and serene,
The essence of Gale, golden and gentle, a fading summer's
dream.
The cooler vibe of Cyrus, a dramatic shift from the heat of
Hawthorn,
Yet warm enough for Tempest to stir the soul's delight, reborn.

Before Lyra fades, just as the sun has risen high,
A magic in Maples stirs beneath the sky.
In that quiet hour, like Rowan, the earth does wake,
And whispers to Autumn, the promise of paths to take.

Sage and Crimson witness as morning dew clings to the
leaves,
Crystal and Willow give way, a sparkle caught in webs
they weave.
Drake comes to Lark, and together in the mist, they drift
slow and wide,
A shroud of mystery, Riley and Briar embark on the
countryside.

In the stillness, to Fern and Skye, the world feels new,
A canvas waiting for the brush to strew.
The coolness of the air invites reflection,
Alder and Gale, welcome Cyrus, in quiet connection.

Lyra gently falls as the first light beckons, calm and clear,
Mystical Maple and Clever Crystal visualize a time to
conquer fear.
Where past and future gently collide,
In the soft glow of the morning tide.

Ekphrasis 4:

Cascading Leaves and Light

Ekphrasis 4:
Cascading
Leaves and Light

Vignette 2

Childhood Whispers

Robin's Beautyberry Bush

Delicate and precious to me, deep are your roots, tall are your stems
Plump and juicy fruit, blankets of streams, scents fill the air, ah but a dream
How I long to experience the taste your luscious, velvety, and alluring resilience
I count the days for your return, spring has recoiled, it's time for Autumn's recurrence

Nevertheless, I adore the Autumn, with is colorful embrace and gentle touch
It's warmth and glow, its passion and flair, its courageous generosity, others misjudge
Long ago, across time and space, I thought often of your return and what if meant to me
Throughout generations lost, I grappled with the memories of my beautyberry bush in all its glory

Beyond legacy and luxury, between the layers of land and see,
Your grace, elegance, class, and beauty is all I see
Not in body nor in deed, not in status nor in grace, no other dare compare to thee
Not in vibrance nor versatility, you are the only one for me

Cyclone's overflowing with your scent, every bird in the air is in love with thee
Yet tis I only that you see
Autumn has reclaimed her love for me and I am lost to you once again, I digress

Imbue the land, ingrained with your expansive opulence, a backdrop filled with harmonious excellence

Eternally I will carry you with me, no matter the distance, the age, or the season
The very thought of you, my mere existence, is the only reason
Incessantly I tell the world of the taboo of our expression
My devotion to only you, written in this confession

Those that remember the fullness of your textured layers
Are enticed by your riveting delicacy and adorableness
The sophistication of your aroma, the appeal draws all acquainted
Debilitated by earth's harsh and cruel demeanor, subtle dispels, your fragrance fainted

Regardless, the tenderness of your touch remains untainted
Our forbidden romance is all but debated
Autumn declares me as her love, yet I declare you as mine
You are my partner forever and for all time.

Autumn's Child

Tender heart, a spark from the start,
Born beneath the Autumn sky,
Where leaves drift like whispers in the crisp air,
A life so bright, emerging from stillness,
A quiet miracle in the Autumn winds.

The world exhales, life stirs, and grows—
Like a newborn's first breath at dawn,
This is the moment everything begins again.
Autumn's embrace cradles you,
A warmth woven in the quiet decay,
A season that promises new life.

You are of the earth, the sky, the falling leaves,
Rooted deep, yet free.
From the soil beneath, you rise—
Nourished by time, and untouched by the past.
In the stillness, you bloom,
A heartbeat tethered to the world's pulse,
Every leaf a story of joy and heartache,
Every breeze carries hopes untold.

In the cool Autumn air,
A life begins, fresh and full of possibility,
An unspoken yearning for peace, for growth,
A story yet to unfold, a soul yet to bloom.
No exchange, only the pure gift of existence,
For in the quiet moments of Autumn,
Life begins again.

Blooms of Autumn

Spring is clear, winter is dark
Summer captures the mundane's heart
Life and death, light to dark
Seasons change, Autumn's first start

Trees will bloom again, granting us grace
Sedum, celosia, viola presents of peace
Scents of Autumn, pumpkin, mandarins, and spice
Sunflowers rising, Calendula bursting bring

My life will never dwindle like the rose or the lily
My love will never fade away from memory
It will have eternal meaning
Autumn's blooms bring and everlasting lovers greeting

Life and death, joy and sorrow
Time is not promised, nor tis tomorrow
Chrysanthemum infused tea comforts me completely
Sweet in stature, the scents of Dahlia linger over me

Between the Leaves

There was a tree in the midland forest planted by the riverbanks of the angelic twin waterfalls.

It pondered often the questions of life, its place and purpose, and many, if not most, of these questions began with why.

It asked, "I'm a vessel, a willing vessel of Autumn, but why does Autumn not know my name?

I am often fearful when winter storms come upon me, fire rages against me, and life is filled with uncertainty. Yet, why does Autumn not send protection to cover me?

I am here all alone while the other creatures of the forest have a companion to call their own.

Yet, why does Autumn not send a connection, a companion, a comforter to me when I'm lonely?

I feel and hurt, I bend and break, I cry and fall. Yet no one comes when I call.

Does a tree in the forest still not make a sound when it falls even when there is no one there to hear?"

Autumn still does nothing, remains silent, doesn't recall.

This tree in the midland forest, planted by the riverbanks of the angelic twin waterfalls, had no idea it had Autumn's ear.

The wind whispers ever so gently,
"I am here at your beckon call when you need someone to
listen."

The owl flies by and sits on its limbs to reply,
"I am here when you need someone to hear you cry."

The squirrel climbs up its trunk to say,
"I'm here to give you comfort today."

The rabbit hops along, singing its beautiful song, letting the
tree know it's not alone.

The tiger and lion both sit underneath the cool breeze its
leaves offer them to let it know that they are there to
protect it from every fear.

And the flowers and the bees inform the tree,
"We know you by name, and the name is known to all the
same.
You are the Tree of Life, a blessing to all, a sight to behold,
a purpose more precious than silver and gold."

Autumn declared your purpose to simply be a sign of hope
for all who believe.

The Tree of Life, now understanding its purpose and place,
was to serve and stand for good.

It realized it was never alone, ignored, or misunderstood.

It was loved, respected, and altogether good.

Autumn's Addiction

Moonlight, rustling leaves, whistling trees, the bellows of the night air, music to my ears

Starlight, cherry drops, blop blop, the rounding sounds of rain drops, tingling my senses

Blackout, cool breezes, gentle teases, creeping crawling little creatures, mythical fears

Tick Tock, sliding hands, gliding fingers, kisses linger, memories together, teeth clinches

Spotlight, times run out, breathless whispers, pounding heartbeats, grasping

Delight, star gazing, blood racing, smells and sensations, borrowed time, endless friction

Slight plot twist and turn, navigate direction, pathway stretching

Twilight, maverick attracts, tenderness, attentiveness, craving confession, Autumn's addiction

Full Bloom Serenade

Hearts racing, melodies to reveal

The harmony of thoughts and emotions,

A tidal wave of rhythmic movements

Soothing harp strings, glistening, whimsically

Lyrical dancing, unwinding touches

Resonating in the hearts of the distant,

Echoing the bellows that only the souls know

Uplifting melancholy, a metamorphosis emboldened

Vibrant as the star filled sky, untouched by the noise

Dissonant dreams of lovers torn

Rich in change, essence embodied in art

Serene in beauty, spectacle of fortune, grace unpolished

Pulsing, hearts racing, feet chasing sighs

Soulful memories, pallets to taste

Lingering flavors only lovers recognize

Enchanting, everlasting, eternal

Full bloom serenade

The Drama of My Life

They say what doesn't kill you makes you stronger

But I was never weak to begin with

You see I'm a champ in my own right

Every challenge overcomes every battle won

You say I'm nothing without you

But I was more before you came into my view

Living this life the only way I can

Standing on my principles speaking real to the man

They say misery loves company

But I can love myself all alone the way I am

I'll never be who you want me to be

So why pretend

This is the drama of my life

To be better than the rest

To maintain the air in our chest

To reach incredible heights

To be brighter than darkness' plight

To bring truth to the light

To speak, shout, scream what's right

They say fake it until you make it

But I'm too real for that

I'm unapologetically me

Totally incredibly undoubtedly free

I may not be your cup of tea

But I don't have to prove my value

Everything I am, say, and due is to real for you

This is the drama of my life

To rise above the rest

To create a world that's free

Where I can continue to be me

To leave a legacy

To bridge ancestry

To create generational wealth

To live long and prosper

To heal spiritual health

I'll cry myself to sleep at night

Yet I'll rise again

Like Ali I'll continue the fight

I'll carry on and win

We all get weary, tired, and stressed

But this is the drama of my life

Our choice to be better than the rest

Dancing Branches

It's you, swaying with the birds, floating with the leaves,
A rhythm only you could play, a song I breathe.
You lift me up and spin me round until breath escapes—
In your embrace, I lose myself, caught in your chase.

It's you, my thoughts forever consumed,
Dreaming, glowing, anticipating, ever entombed.
It's you—your arrival, flawless as always,
My grace, my daze, caught in a craze.

Run away, blaze, my heart can't keep pace,
I need you more than you need me,
A tragic truth, but I can't break free.
This love affair, evening wear, dancing branches
everywhere.

It's you, as it always has been, always will be,
As if any others could ever stand a chance against you and
me.
I turn to you, I yearn for you, I cry for you,
My soul dances, forever drawn to you.

But will this love last, or fade like the fall?
Time will tell, but I'm yours through it all.

Mountaintop

When I see you looking back at me, I wonder what it is you
truly see
Do you see through me, the days of Adam and Eve
Do you see the pain and the agony
Do you see the horror and tragedy
What is it that you see

Mirror mirror on the wall who's the greatest of them all
Not Summer, not Winter, nor Spring answers the call
Autumn, in all its wonder, splendor, and beauty, better
known as Fall
Summer has heat, Winter has snow, Spring has raindrops
the size of baseballs
But my friend Autumn has the vibrance of hues that
soothes the soul and warms the hearts' walls

Standing outside the post office watching you watching me
The changing colors of the leaves greet me
The aromas of cinnamon and spice, the glimpse of yellow
glory from the willow tree
Not a cloud in the sky, tear drops from my eyes, whispers of
melancholy
I miss you, the thought and sight of you, the warmth and
smell of you, don't you see

When I see you looking back at me, I wonder what it is you
truly see
Jasmine in Winter, overshadowing the bedrock of the
frozen sea
Roses with thorns in Spring, the butterfly, or bumble bee

Tulips or lilies in hottest days of Summer, beware the leaves of three
Orange marmalade, luxurious olive shade, crimson crossing passageways, Autumn's finale

Changing Colors

And so it begins, as it often does, with a shift of scene,
Jade enters, setting the tone, with glamour and a dream.
Scarlet takes the stage, draped in elegance and grace,
While Ember's fiery copper hue ignites the space.
But wait — there's more, the guest of honor's near,
Autumn's finest, just about to appear.

Sunlight drifts, moonlight veils, evening tide embraces the next,
Porcelain and tropical mist — calm and bliss, the evening's quest.
Toffee and butterscotch, sweetness wrapped in velvety delight,
Pleasure refined, lavender's ethereal glow dances in the night.
Amethyst, it must be you, circling, ever so sly,
A game of chance, pleasing every eye.

Still waiting for the guest of honor, who could it be? A guessing game,
Mauve, Violet, or Chartreuse, with their zest and playful fame?
The evening's still young, and dinner's on the way,
A hush fills the room as the bell begins to play.
Take your seats, the feast will soon unfold,
The maître d' speaks, the tale now told.

Old world glow, Pewter's gleam — warm and refined,
Mercury and Birch, in perfect time aligned.
Yet the guest of honor has yet to appear,
First course is served, silver gleams, crystal clear.
The table set, nothing less than Silver Lining's best,

A feast for the senses, a true moment of rest.

Has the guest of honor finally arrived?
Which Autumn hue has risen, the most prized?
The color that proves its depth and might,
A twilight sky reflects its light.

Glistening, iridescent, raven feathers glimmer in
moonlight,
Royal shade, deep and rich, the epitome of noble height.
Onyx, smooth as silk, meets its match tonight,
Rising through the ranks, the evening's true delight.

Mystery, elegance, and strength define,
Exuding transformation, protection, all intertwined.
Midnight's crown jewel, iconic and true,
Rise and welcome — Ebony, we honor you.

Evening Tide

There is this sense of luminous reflective moonlight
whispering across candlelight
Soothing chilly bearings of lost gentleness dancing in the
wilderness
Mellow as the memories rippling through time
Tranquil rustling of Autumn's leaves leaving a trail for the
bling
Soft moonlit mushrooms widen the trails
Smoky glimmering lights from twilights and ringing bells
Shimmering eerie snowballs and cottontails
Dusk-tinged ashes crashed upon the land
Whoever thought the sight of the evening tide would be a
peaceful view
Timeless enchanted essence, twilights morning dew
Crisp and serene, the cool gentle breeze
Dreamy, starry, timing is everything
Faintly fragrant, moonlit whispering
Evening tide is calling, beckoning, come to me.

Autumn of Innocence

Mulled in the pure, childlike fog of my mind

Smoldering in the crisp foliage of time

Autumnal spice, roasted chestnut, moss-covered earth

Caramelized sugar on woodsmoke in the warmth of
unsullied touch

Fallen leaves, damp soil, the earth personified, its soul
unspoiled

Sweetened pine, crisp apples, toasted pumpkin, and thyme

Simple, honest, soft and kind

Cinnamon bark in its roughest part, blameless in its blight

Crisp foliage, fresh and naive, radiant in its trusting serene
views

Amber warmth, sweet and vibrant, tranquil morning dew

Golden warm earthy rustling of beautiful Autumn leaves

Untouched, unbiased, quiet in every memory

Brisk in the midst of colorful mist

Innocence in essence,

Autumn's blessing

Ekphrasis 5:

Nature's Tapestry

HEY
chay
Ekphrasis 5:
Nature's
Tapestry

Vignette 3

The Tides of Adolescence

Love Discovered

Dear Autumn,

I used to wonder what it would be like to finally fall in love
Now I am certain that there is no such thing as falling in love
If you can fall in love, you can certainly fall out of love
No, love is more simple and yet more complex than one can ever imagine

Love is something you grow into over time
It's something that you do, not just say
Love is in fact an action word; you have to work hard to obtain and maintain it
I never thought love would be so dramatic, so difficult, and yet so easy and so whimsical

Love is a word that describes not just a feeling or an emotion
But dedication and a devotion to something greater than one's self
Love is a lifelong aspiration, it is evolution realized, it is magical in every sense of the word
It's pure and passionate, filled with the still silence of the night and the musical moments of stars dancing at twilight

Love is as scary as it is real
Love is blind to all things negative, and open to all things possible and positive
Love is timeless and rare, priceless and bare, eternal and everywhere
Love is who we are and what we are meant to be, say, and do

Love is your true north guiding you
Love is encapsulating
Love is, was and will always be
Seen, experienced, shared, expressed, eternally

I have been fortunate for I have had love surrounding me
all the days of my life
Even when I felt utterly alone, I knew I was loved, when I
was sad and lonely
I knew I was loved, when I was heartbroken and filled with
anger, I knew I was loved
Most importantly, when I felt loveless and unable to love, I
knew I was loved.

It is love that keeps us, strengthens us, moves & motivates
us
It is love that fills us, uplifts us, empowers & guides us
Love directs us, fulfills us, and gives us purpose
It is love that gives this life meaning and value, love that
cleanses and purifies us

Priceless, timeless, eternal
Love grows and develops and builds character
Love has the power to build entire communities,
strengthen families
Connect strangers, end wars, heal the brokenhearted,
recover the lost, solve mysteries, and discover endless
possibilities

I was once lost, walking the earth aimlessly, without
direction, without purpose
Not knowing where I would end up or what I would
become
Life was something I did, not something I lived

Yes, I loved my family, and yes, they loved me, yet I had a
hole that was unable to be filled by their love

A loneliness that was subsequent to despair
Then one glorious day, in the midst of the chaos that was
my life and the world around me, love found me
My sweetheart, my king, my love, my future, my purpose,
my center, he discovered me
Blessed beyond measure, I now live peacefully & happily.

Crimson Leaves

Urban parks, sparks, flames. Maples, oaks, and sumacs dressed in vibrant crimson, gold, and amber. A creative delicacy of exuberant accelerating exquisite tapestry. The vibrance felt across acres of forests, hillsides, and endless fields, and bottomless valleys. Carpeted with fallen crimson leaves, Autumn's way of softening the earth, a bed of fellows, crafting a bold rhythm of movement through eclectic colors.

The potency once felt in the lush greens of bustling trees now replaced by the fiery beauty of crimson leaves. Marigold orange, and apple candy corn, a representation of time passing, distance crashing, nothing is everlasting. Crimson leaves flutter gently, swirling in the breeze, filling the air with impending change.

Crimson leaves caught in a gust of wind, twisting and spinning through the air before landing on the ground. Once again, the ending is the beginning, in death, life can once again be found. Only in the shedding of the old can one make way for the new.

Crimson leaves capture the bittersweet beauty of letting go, captivate the senses, allowing the age of time to follow through. Allowing and granting permission for this period in life to once again be filled with vitality and energy. An overwhelming sense of rebirth and renewal.

Remember once again, evoking feelings of deep love, fierce dedication, or even anger. A sign that crimson leaves do not fade into the darkness of winter's background. Yet it demands and retains the attention it has fought to gain.

And in life, as in death, are these symbolic and nostalgic moments. Where we are most engaged with our inner selves. Where we feel most alive, and our hearts, minds, and souls thrive.

September Autumn

The aroma of freshly baked sweet potato pie fills the air, the scent mingling with the cool breeze of Autumn. The rocking chair creaks gently on the porch, a quiet moment of reflection on days gone by. The breeze carries the familiar fragrances of pine, pumpkin, and cinnamon, each scent evoking memories etched deeply in time. September has always been a month of transformation—a time of beginnings and endings, of quiet shifts and moments of revelation.

September brought the earliest lessons of care and resilience. It was in this month that the seeds of purpose were planted. In its embrace, one learned that every stage of life, every challenge, was an invitation to grow stronger, to rise, and to become who one was always meant to be.

Autumn, with its shifting colors and unpredictable winds, was a time of change, a season that has shaped countless generations. Its lessons are timeless. It is both a guide and a muse, providing wisdom to those who are willing to listen. It is the keeper of the past, the teacher of the present, and the herald of what is to come.

In September of 1999, a challenge arose—one that would forever change the course of life. A premature birth, a miracle against all odds, was a lesson in strength and survival. Against the weight of uncertainty, faith was tested, and a deep love emerged, capable of conquering any fear. From this moment forward, purpose became clear: to nurture, to protect, and to love with an unwavering heart.

The years that followed taught the importance of service, of sacrifice, and of standing firm in the face of life's storms. Leadership was never sought but embraced, not as a title but as a responsibility to those who depended on it. September was a constant reminder of this truth: it is not the absence of challenge that defines one's path, but the willingness to face it head-on.

Autumn, with its golden light and fading warmth, has always been a reminder that change is inevitable, yet beautiful. It is a warrior, a lover, and a friend. Through every trial, every passion, and every purpose fulfilled, it guides and strengthens those willing to walk its path. In the fire of life, strength is forged. In struggle, character is built.

As the years pass, the lessons learned in September continue to resonate. The journey, shaped by both hardship and grace, becomes a testament to resilience. In the quiet moments of reflection, the truth is clear: though the road has been long and the weight heavy, there is strength in perseverance. Every obstacle, every dream pursued, has led to this moment—a legacy forged through love, service, and unwavering faith.

Today, as the seasons shift once again, the story of September remains a living testament to the power of purpose. Each step taken has been part of a greater design, a journey toward fulfillment. And in that fulfillment, a life is celebrated—not just for the triumphs, but for the lessons learned along the way.

Shifting Sands

Shifting sand can be seen everywhere you go. In the golden hues of desert dunes and in the criss-crossed paths, tracks from crabs, birds, or other beach creatures all along the coast. Erosion and sedimentation in constant consistent motion. Where water wears away at the edges of the riverbanks, forever altering the landscape, forming new beaches, islands, or even shifting coastlines and shrinking oceans.

Shifting sands, parting seas, shrinking lands, burning trees. Impermanence, change, and uncertainty take away from nature's profound beauty. Autumn's landscape, in a constant state of flux, shifting gears is a must. What happened to the reverence we once had, and the trust is now all but lost. What happened to the loyalty we once revered, and now lies is all we have. Now magnified by a shallow view of sand grains shifting under the influence of a tiny breeze, catapulted to new heights it was never to hold. Truth, sadness, undoubtedly to unfold.

Small ripples form, now tidal waves overtake us, causing sandy storms. As water flows over sandy soil, damp earth, causing a great shift, nature splits. Unwanted divide, the evening tide, lawlessness ensues, honesty defied. Integrity departed. Replaced by disdain. The sound of minute grains moving the sand. The stillness of the air drops the temperature at night, undercover covert affairs, and scandalous plots. The moonlight casts long shadows across the desert dunes, enemies of the state, and war pursues.

Shifting sands, where will it end? The imprints of footfalls might be erased or altered by morning, but the lasting corrosiveness will be felt ongoing. A landscape that is never static, ever-changing, means we're always alone. The transitory nature of existence, the quiet yet unstoppable forces of nature at work.

Shifting sands, surreal in their feel, slowly changing the scape and scope of the earth. Sightless is not unseen, heartless is not unfelt, hurting is not imagined, and although you can't see it, the changes are still happening. Ignorance is not bliss, tackles in tone. Autumn's unfolding, bolding, holding, scolding. Shifting sands, serve as a final warning.

Midnight Moments

Knock. Knock. The sounds of tree branches knocking on my
front door.
Bustling winds send whistling sounds you can move to on the
dance floor.
Rocking chair creeks, crackling sounds of the roaring
fireplace sending hues of orange and red throughout the
living room,
Comfy old sofa with a special dent in it just for you
Curved to fit your body ever so perfectly, enjoying the
midnight view

The warmth of my bed is calling my name, but the winds
and the tree tops are doing the same
Which shall I answer, which shall I go to
Melancholy moments, midnight dreams, tabletop dances,
jazz band sings
Piano keys are moving, footsteps are grooving, drum beats,
tree leaves, captivating me

Ever sit in your house, on your sofa, in your bed
Took a moment, when its quiet and there's nothing being
said
Seemingly in constant motion and feeling overwhelmed
Feel out of control a little crazy, ah enough said

Dance the night away in your wedding dress
Sway and swing, glide across your bedroom in your
birthday suit
No worries about tomorrow, no feelings of being
undervalued
No pressure from the world climbing down on top of you

No feelings of sadness, depression, or despair
No thoughts or concerns about feeling alone
Ups and downs and endless battles of life and the craziness
of this world
No one said it would be easy, no one dared said a word

My friend you are not alone
Autumn is calling for you to carry on
She loses a piece of herself and yet manages to still move
on
Never once waiting a moment to sing, to dang, to play
along

How much more can you take, you won't know until you
go through
More importantly, you won't know until after you've gone
through
What makes Autumn so sweet is her precious memories
Of love and laughter and generosity

What makes Autumn so beautiful are the colors she
presents
All the amazing adventures because of it
Hues of beige, green and gold sprout forth fortune untold
Glistenings of lime, red, and rose breathes essence of all to
behold

So dance and shout, sing and scream
Do the unthinkable, be whatever you want to be
Autumn's true value is not what she gives or gets
It's what she's always done in the midnight moments, she
persists

Harvest Moon

The fields are ripe with passion, aroma fills the air with the essence of their inner beauty, glistens of sweet nothings, doubts, and despairs. It is time, Rowan and I, to catch and ride the evening tide, to meet the lovers of Rosemary and Thyme.

To captivate and circulate the cotton and twine. To motivate and activate the cinnamon, sugar, spice, and mahogany butterscotch, it's almost harvest time.

The moon, in all its wonderful splendor, greets us at the door, lovers no more, winter's knocking on the door, once more, the one who we adore, departs in silence. Harvest time means an end to one season and the beginning of another, farewell to a friend, hello to a lover.

Acquaintances once more, broomsticks meet the floor. Garden, your time has ended. We have no more room at the inn. The stars are all here, and the planets are around the bend.

No more sky-filled romantic notions. No more rowing, rolling, tossing in the ocean. Harvest moon comes through and with it, you know who! Sue and Nomi, Tidal and Wave. Say goodbye to Hawthorne and Maple, Crimson, Cyrus, and Sage. Say hello to Frost, Tempest, and Drake.

These are the days of our lives, enemies now bedfellows, husbands and wives. The harvest moon darkens our door once more, and now that it's arrived, who knows what's in store.

What's In a Name

It was once said, a rose by any other name is still a rose —
But Shakespeare stole that from me, I suppose.
Cherished by the colors of my fields,
The blues of my oceans, the hues of my skies —
He dares to claim this notion,
But let me tell you the true story, if you'll lend me your ear.

A lover and a friend, conquered by time,
A fleeting end, yet fate would not decline.
Seeking a way out, the stars held the key,
And thus began the plot, destined to be.
The star-crossed lovers, in Shakespeare's tale,
Find an ill-gotten fate, their love doomed to fail.

But the truth of the story, beyond his pen,
Is one of romance, of kismet, again and again.
The potion, the dagger, the twisting of fate,
Could not sever the bond they'd come to create.
It would only delay until they met once more,
For the lover and the friend would live, not implore.

In the forest, in the trees, in the stars in the sky,
In the oceans and seas, where the echoes don't die,
They'd journey far, beyond the reach of strife,
To a distant land where love would come to life.
Enemies, foes, and naysayers left behind,
Never again would they tarnish what was destined to
shine.

The lies foretold in the story of old —
Necessary for survival, or so they were told.
Written by one, once thought an ally,

Now reviled as a rival, with his reasons denied.
Shakespeare, too, plays his unwilling part,
To protect the love, the bond, the heart.

The Seconds In Between

Autumn has arrived, oh how I missed my sweet and
precious friend
I am reminded of a story I want to share, so stick with me
until the end
It's about the parallel of time and space
No, it's about the parallel of birds and snakes

Yet it can also be said it about woman and man
About boy and girl, time and time again
It's not hard to follow, so let us begin
Remember to stick with me until the very end

Some friendships are meant to last a lifetime
Others are meant to last for years
Some are meant to last only briefly
Others will never last and only bring tears
Some are not friendships at all, but something more sinister
Others become more than a good friendship and later
require a minister

In all relationships, there is a beginning and an end
but what lasts for all eternity is what heaven sends
We are connected through purpose, time, and space
We are connected as both spiritual beings and as part of the
human race

If we all remembered one simple fact, God created us all,
it's as simple as that
Love each other, no matter the ups and downs
Time won't always allow us to be around
Forgive that which has past, forge towards a peaceful
future and a new beginning

Give thanks for times of hardship and praise for times of
plenty
Live life not from day to day, but minute by minute
It's in the seconds in between that you will most remember
and treasure
Yet simultaneously it's the easiest to lose and forget forever

So, what did you think of the story, was it good or was it
good
I know what you're thinking, I hope to not be
misunderstood
The simple moral of the story is clear for all to understand
I'm so very happy and thankful, Autumn has returned, my
sweet and precious friend

Remix Melody

Remix melody, I imagine goes something like this. Romaine is invited along with Arugula, Spinach, and Lemon Twist. But what about Zest, aren't we forgetting Spice? Ring the doorbell twice. There is a party underway, and all are invited to come.

This is the last hooray, a charade gone wrong. We forgot about Bell and Pepper, Olive and Big Cheese, my friend from way back when. I remember those mighty Panthers, undefeated and undercounted, best crew around, solid, upstanding, always ready to lift a helping hand. Secure in stature, wandering the garden paths; elevated by grace, always ready, any time, any place.

Remix melody, goes a little something like this, evening shades, and morning bliss. Cotton candy clouds, squishy squash, and yellow tails, all are invited, the season upheld. We dance and sing, laugh and cry, our lives forever intertwined, in this garden of mine.

Autumn, we love your beat, your rhythm is ultra smooth, your vibes are out of this world, and gives a cool groove. Who knew you were such a cool cat, a romanticist at that! Remix melody, now that's where it's at!

Stripped Away

It is in our darkest moments,
The lights go out,
The sky turns pale,
The tear drops begin to fall
And the flood from the rain rises.

It is in these moments,
Our voices cry out but are silent,
Our inner temperature rises yet we are cold,
Our mind races yet it is empty.

It is in these moments our friends are lost to us,
Are family is estranged from us,
And we are all alone in the world.
It is in these moments we discover what we are made of.

It is in these moments our strength
Comes from something greater
And more powerful than us.

It is in these moments we must dig deep
Come to terms with who we truly are at our core.
Do you know who you are?
I do.

Autumn's Solo

Autumn's solo happens after all our friends have departed. What a wonderful time had by all, the memory will last a lifetime and then some. Autumn takes one last glance over, cleans up the space, and takes time to wonder, a song comes to heart. A solo.

The breeze blowing through branches or rustling through tall grasses adds a fluid tone, the soft padding of a rabbit and the squirrel darting through the underbrush give way to the beat of a drum.

The plants themselves don't make a sound, their presence felt in this garden of mine, signifies a swaying moment enhanced through color and texture, as each enjoys Autumn's graceful melody.

The hum of bees, the fluttering of butterflies, and the distant buzz of dragonflies provide the harmony, a beautiful melancholy. Autumn's solo is no solo at all. Yet it exudes hues, displaying a symphony of life that is constantly evolving.

Showcasing a delicate balance between tranquility and vitality, with every element playing its part to create an organic, harmonious whole. Autumn's solo is its gift to the rest of us.

A reminder of the fragility of life, blind faith, and trust. Captivated by the moments, seconds, tender mercy afforded to us. Never forgotten, life departed, life lived, eternal, blessed, nature's syllabus.

Whispers Left Behind

Whispers left behind. Blinded to the very end. No one told me how to say goodbye or where to begin. Our story is a love affair that will surely surpass the test of time. A story of belonging. A story of glory. A story to end all stories. A story, no, a testimony.

Our love isn't one of a kind, because there is none like yours, none like mine. It doesn't exist in this cold dark world. Filled with endless critics and unkind words. No, a love like ours is not allowed to exist. It dares to reset the ills of resistance. Unfathomed in the end, a retaliation to circumvent the status quo.

No. Our love is not one of a kind, because there is none like yours, none like mine. It is our life's journey, the work of our souls. It is what we dared to tell our children, the ones we never got to hold. It is the love of generations, lost to history's mysteries and false revelations.

It is a story that can only be told in silence, felt in the wind, smelled in the rain, craved in the pain. It is something so tyrannical, a force that is welcomed when nothing else exists outside of itself. It is a calamity, a tragedy, and spirituality.

No. Our love is not one of a kind, because there is none like yours, none like mine. Lost through time and space. Beloved by mercy and grace. Written all in one place. Seen on your face, mistake. Replace.

Smiles can no longer be found. Songs of laughter, no longer sound. The frantic tones in the voices of the wonderless. A tragic plot twist. No. Our love is one of a kind because there is none like yours, none like mine. As Autumn comes and goes, so shall we in the whispers left behind.

Ekphrasis 6:

Autumn's Essence Whispered

HEY
chay
Ekphrasis 6:
Autumn's Essence
Whispered

Ekphrasis 7:

Ocher Reverie

HEY
chay
Ekphrasis 7:
Ocher Reverie

Vignette 4

Echoes of Youth

Autumn's Eternal Love

Autumn has shown me what I don't want in love, I don't want to fall

Come to think if it, isn't is a ridiculous notion

To fall, means eventually you will get hurt, and then what

Autumn has taught me how to love in layers, in colors, in depth, and in waves

Autumn has shown me even when the leaves fall, it makes room for growth

I want to grow into love, over and over again, desperately seeking it eternally

Love is something that sprouts change

It constantly and consistently evolves into something more than before

Autumn has taught me what I want to have in love

A love that unfolds in layers over time and in stages

A love that will be timeless and survive the ages

Autumn has shown me that I need to welcome change and embrace growth

Love build, develops, and becomes stronger over time

Autumn has taught me the blessing of what an eternal love truly means and can be

Friendships can last forever as is or ripen in to a beautiful romance

Strangers can become acquaintances, then friends, and eventually lovers

Autumn has shown me what love can become

Love can, like the magnolia, blossom under any circumstance, if given a chance

It can be written in the hearts of men and sung by the tongues of everyone

I want not just an epic romance but a triumphant victory dance

Autumn has taught me what true love really is and what it certainly is not

Love is not fast or loose, it's not always easy to spot and can be easily missed

It can be overlooked, misunderstood, and eventually, unwillingly, potentially lost

Love is patient, kind, passionate, enduring, hopeful, and blind

Love is more than deep desire, beyond want and need

Love is everything God truly intended it to be

Autumn has shown me what Love can reveal

Love can breathe understanding, cleanse wounds, and heal

Love is not what is written in some of the fictitious Fad writings of novelist

Love is a story yet to unfold in my deepest heart of hearts, yet hope to be told

Autumn has taught me to be the author of my love own story

Love is not to be sold, but passed down, & reviled upon for generations to come

I want a love that can only be screamed from the rooftops and shared in a whisper

I want a love that can be seen clearly from the mountain tops, derived from heaven

Autumn shown and taught me so very much

Autumn, only now I see how much you mean to me and I mean to you

Innamorarsi

Sunrise has come, time for the lovers to meet

Most would gather under the cover of darkness, but ours is a

love so sweet

The steps taken to meet you are treasured deep in my soul

Your eyes I pine to see, your arms I crave to be in, your hands

I long to hold

Inamorato, the wind calls out for thee

Inamorata, replies the long stim branches full of golden

locks of leaves on the willow tree

Before I saw you in the flesh, you visited me in my dreams

Singing as you paddled across the wide river stream

The song of bliss, ah, I shall never forget

Expressions of love, longing, and Limerence

Pressing my way forward, I sing the same melody

Passing through bushes and trees

Covered in grand colors of gold, ruby, ginger and beyond

these

Flowers of passion, fruits of desire, birds of contentment,

nature's on fire

Inamorato, the birds chirp loudly

Inamorata, replies the owl of destiny

Delana, I am coming for thee, please wait patiently

Tis the first time I heard you call my name out loud

I rushing feeling of warmth was bursting deep inside

Delana, my love, can you hear my voice

I wanted to cry tears of joy, with a smile on my face,

running through the forest

Delana, my sweetheart come quickly

My pace picks up ever so swiftly

The melody of the trees, the wind seemed to carry me

The footsteps grow closer, I am almost there, I tell my feet

to hurry

Delana, my darling, forever and always, I shall be with you

for the rest of our days

No, throughout the eternities, our love will continue to

grow, forever and always

On the horizon, what do my eyes see, Inamorato, my

darling, my forever Steve

I leap over streams, and cross over valleys, climb

mountains, beyond what one would believe

I would travel the world to get to thee, I would scour the

globe over to be with you

Innamorarsi, to fall in love with you, over and over again,

my dream come true

Midnight Plea

In the middle of the night, I think of you.

With the smell of the rain drops, and the smoothness of the morning dew

I cannot help but wonder if you think of me as I do you

If your attention is curved or if you crave the attention of the same

If your eyes but rise up to the level of that which you seek

You will find all that you hold dear, but at last you are too weak

You are tempted by that which you do not yet understand

One wrong step, all that you hold so close will be swept from the land

And so I give you fair warning of your crimes

Behold the nature of the beast, the battle in your own mind

You know that which you do, is wrong and still you go

You know that which you touch is not for you to hold

You know that which you see, is not for your very eyes

You know the tales you tell, are nothing but foolish lies

Beware that which you take for granted will always be there

For one day you will open your eyes and nothing will be spared

Take this time to reflect that which you have caused great harm

Take this moment to reject that which you know is wrong

Take this second chance you have to repent of sinners' past

Take the breath and life you have to build that which will last

Call the name of which will heal, will, hold, will comfort, and will save

Release the stronghold that the dark one has used to make you his slave

Call upon and bow to the one who's name is above all

Jesus Christ, the almighty son, upon which all shall call

Holy, righteous, savior to child, woman, and man

The one and only way to God, to return to heaven again.

Endless Whispers

Breathless as I approach your sweet embrace

Still fragment of subtle serenity

Fresh and purse, crisp and clean

I faint at the thought of your echo-less eternal heart

Empty and cool, soft velvety hollow frost

Tranquil, ethereal, timeless whisper

The clarion call comes for us all

Clear thoughts, blank stares, shrouded in moonlit stairs

A hush rides the wind, infinite and unfathomable, friend

Velvet untouched dewy sage

Frozen lullabies, clouded in misguided waves

Distant, boundless, timeless as the sky

Unseen luminous wind-swept leaves

Celestial ethereal vast dreams

Cosmic solitary, a game best played

By the endless whispers of Autumn's serenade

Autumn's Dream

In whispers of white and silver light,
A tapestry of color unfurls —
The wedding dress, a crimson flame,
Against the Autumn's soft embrace.

Platinum tuxes, sleek and bright,
The bridal party in a shimmering dance,
Red and white accents flicker,
Like leaves caught in a fleeting glance.

Beneath the grand oaks, where shadows play,
Guests arrive, all clad in white,
As laughter mingles with the crisp air,
In a garden of memories, pure and light.
Music drifts like falling leaves,
With digital notes weaving through,
Three hours under the pavilions' shade,
As love blooms anew.

A simple feast, flavors entwined,
Crab cakes and salmon, a savory delight,
Desserts piled high, sweet dreams await,
As mocktails glimmer in the fading light.

No phones to capture the moment's grace,
Disposable memories shared and embraced,
A digital booth, laughter contained,
In this Autumn reverie, love remains.

And as the sun dips low,
In hues of amber and gold,
Family gathers, hearts entwined,
Celebrating a bond that's bold.

In the echoes of laughter,
In the rustle of leaves,
Autumn weaves its magic,
As love takes flight, and time believes.

The Lost Lake

In Autumn's breath, where whispers twist,
a haze of golden curls meets mist,
ginger roots lie buried deep,
their warmth is a promise for dreams to keep.

A peppermint breeze, soft and slow,
curling through the leaves below,
soothes the stomach's ache, so tight,
and chases off the fading light.

Chamomile blooms in quiet grace,
as aches of body find their place
within the arms of tender tea,
a lullaby of remedy.

Lemon balm, with a touch so mild,
stills the tremor of the wild,
against the chill, its balm will pour,
relief as soft as falling ashore.

Turmeric, golden, slips through dusk,
wrapped in milk, it leaves a trust —
a healing warmth, a tender light,
to soothe the pain before the night.

In the stillness of a lost lake's glow,
where waters rise and fall below,
the herbs of Autumn weave their tale,
in every leaf, in every gale.

Rain Drops in Autumn

When I hear the raindrops fall, I know I'm home
Autumn and the rain, beckoning me to return once again
Drip, drop, tapping at my window, greeting me at my door
Autumn's love, welcoming calling for me once more
lover come on inside, Autumn declares, depart no more

When I hear the raindrops fall, I know who's coming home
Autumn's special surprise brings hope, springs eternal, a
silent calm to the storm
Dinner waiting on the table, for my lover and I
Autumn's first fruits, marmalade, hot apple cider, ginger,
and spices

When I hear the rain drops falling, I know there's no more
reason to cry
Autumn's first choice breads a coffee house vide
Fireside kindling, cracking, sparks fly
The rain begins to stop, the sun comes out to shine

When I hear the snow begin to fall, see the leaves fade to
brown, teardrops begin
The end is near, the earth is clothed in white, winter has
returned once again
Autumn's packing up and getting ready to depart
Silence is overtaken from the sounds of this poor brown girl's
breaking heart

When I hear the jingle bells ring loudly in the streets
The sleds appear and Christmas music is on repeat
Autumn has already given up, his head no longer held high, I
begin to cry
The time has come for my lover and I to say goodbye.

Melancholy

Webster describes it as a state of deep sadness or a gloomy
mood
I just simply refer to it as Autumn having an attitude
It weeps and moans
Whales in undertones
It cries out endlessly, and suddenly it comes to a halt
I mean really, what is this all about

Why can't we just enjoy a simple stroll in the park
Or go out dancing after dark
Bask in the glow of the rising sun
Spend our time, you know, having fun
Bailing out at the last minute
The signs were all there, I should have seen it

Afraid to commit to one dinner date
Scare it will seal your fate
Past relationships run you crazy
Autumn, are you just being lazy
I do not appreciate you wasting my time
If I was a drinking person, I'd drink 99 bottles of wine

Melancholy, which means black bile
Is just a reminder that Autumn is juvenile
With this crazy attitude
I am just not in the mood
No excuses will I dare accept nor shall I provide
I think our moment has gone and it's time to say goodbye

It's times like these that make me just say 'O!
Farwell, adios, Au revoir, Ciao
There are over twenty ways to say I'm out!

This was your last time, your only shot
It's not my fault you dropped the ball
Don't you dare attempt to call

Secret Garden

In the hush of the dawn, where whispers softly flow,
Abenaki spirits greet the day, as Autumn's colors glow.
Crimson leaves dance lightly, a tapestry unfolds,
While Sioux tales of the Great Plains in gentle breezes are
told.

Underneath the harvest tree, Choctaw hands reach wide,
Gathering nature's bounty, with Lumbee by their side.
Seneca songs rise like smoke, drifting into the air,
Their ties to sacred earth, a reminder of the care.

In this garden of transition, where every leaf is gold,
Ute winds sing stories, as the seasons turn bold.
Cree festivals abound, a celebration of the yield,
Chippewa voices echo, their legacy revealed.

Crisp air wraps around me, a blanket of the land,
Moonstone gleams like silver, Autumn's gentle hand.
Obsidian shadows linger, whispers of the past,
While flint and iron remind us, the seasons hold steadfast.

As I wander through the colors of copper, gold, and rust,
With topaz hues reflecting, the warmth of Autumn's trust.
Bismuth's vibrant crystals glint, like sunsets on the ground,
While tiger's eye and jasper keep the earth's lore profound.

Fireside gatherings echo, in the heart of sacred lands,
Resilience in each moment, as nature understands.
Cycles of life unfolding, with every breath I take,
In this secret garden, where the earth's heart beats awake.

Osage wisdom whispers, as the leaves begin to fall,
Navajo prayers linger, in the coolness of it all.

Pawnee hearts beat proudly, in the glow of harvest's grace,
And Dakota's bonds of friendship find their rightful place.

In this vibrant tapestry, the spirits of the past,
Guide me through this garden, where memories are cast.
With each step, I honor, the paths that led me here,
In the secret garden's embrace, the Autumn sky is clear.

The Center

In the quiet hum of fading light,
maps unfold, rivers drawn in dust,
threads of gold weave into the sky —
a flicker of places we must pass through.

A border hums its distant call,
unseen but felt beneath our feet,
the passport flutters like Autumn leaves,
softly weighted by the unspoken.

A visa, a gate, a whispered rule,
the world spins outward, bending edges —
we trace the lines, once a path,
now a circle, an endless echo.

The stars align without permission,
the center a pulse of ancient breath,
we cross the boundaries —
then return again,
forever revolving.

Where distance meets the heart's thread,
we are both here and there,
woven between the map's soft folds,
held in place by the turning sky.

Indian Trail

Encounter
Beneath a canopy of crimson and amber glow,
I walk the Indian Trail, where ancient stories flow.
Whispers of wind brush through the golden leaves,
Carrying the echoes of elders' stories.
For most, history remains a mystery,
The wind in the trees, tapestry robust.
The path of history, living, breathing, surrounding us,
Hidden in passages, fragments of the past, In God We
Trust.

Encapture
Crisp air wraps around me, a blanket of the season,
As I tread softly on sacred lands, rich with reason.
The vibrant colors dance, a nature's tapestry,
Yet decaying leaves hint at life's deep mystery.
The Cherokee remind me of amber leaves and topaz skies,
Iroquois and Hopi with peaceful citrine hues, mahogany
eyes.
Dakota, the eager and loving friend,
The Navajo, loyal to the very end.

Encouraged
I pause by a harvest tree, its bounty at my feet,
Resilience in its branches, as seasons gently meet.
The fireside gatherings echo in the air,
Where indigenous wisdom teaches love and care.
The Zuni's expertise ensures our harvest thrives,
Pawnee see glorious bismuth sunsets with their luminous
tiger eyes.

Jasper and copper reflect the Omaha dialect,
The Nez Perce, nature's perfect Autumn architect.

Engaged
I feel the spirits of the earth, guiding every step,
In this transitional beauty, where past and present blend.
Each footfall tells a tale, a trail of history,
A cycle of life unfolding, embracing sacred harmony.
Aluminum and moonstone, gifts from the Shoshone,
Malachite and lapis lazuli, long-lost legacies of the Lumbee.
The Choctaw and Sioux, covered land rich in carnelian,
silver, and flint,
Cree and Ute, spiritual gifts, heaven's scents, Autumn's
descent.

Evolved
Your gifts you freely gave, made all the difference,
From onyx and tin to roaming flocks and folds, it's evident.
So we remember those who lived before the great fall:
Osage, Ojibwe, Abenaki, we heed your call.
As I walk this path, my heart is full and wide,
For the bounty of the land is a cherished guide.
With every breath I take, I honor what's been,
Along this Indian Trail, where I truly begin.

Just Beyond the Juniper Tree

Just beyond the Juniper tree

As twilight drapes the land in blue,
Sage whispers secrets, soft and true.
With leaves of gold and a gentle sigh,
A majestic creature glides on by.

The closer you come, the taller it is.

Lark flutters near with a song so bright,
Her melodies dance in the cool, crisp night.
She sees the guest in a cloak of red,
With sparkling eyes where stars are bred.

The Juniper tree calls your name.

"Who is this traveler?" Skye wonders aloud,
As the forest gathers, both curious and proud.
The Harvest Fest glimmers with feasts and cheer,
But mystery lingers; the night draws near.

Evening shines through the leaves of the Juniper tree.

"Let's uncover the truth," Sage proposes with grace,
"Invite him to join in this magical space."
Lark flutters closer, her heart full of light,
As the fairies prepare for a wondrous night.

Juniper tree, scents of radiance in the air

But when the guest declines their toast with care,
Whispers of doubt float through the air.

Lark's voice, a melody, breaks the tense hush,
"Who are you to refuse us? Don't make us rush!"

A perfect hiding place, the Juniper tree, standing grace

With confidence shining, the creature replies,
"I am but myself, beneath these starry skies."
His words weave a spell, capturing their gaze,
As Skye feels the thrill of the unfolding maze.

In the garden forest, the Juniper tree reigns supreme.

He speaks of a quest from a king far away,
To find a fair princess and invite her to play.
Sage and Lark, filled with wonder, agree,
To embark on a journey, as magical as can be.

The Juniper tree, ever a mystery

Through shimmering woods where secrets abound,
They arrive at a palace, where joy can be found.
With treasures like rubies and rivers of gold,
The air hums with laughter, stories untold.

The king of the land, could not forge a perfect hand where
Juniper stands.

At the top of the stairs, the king stands so grand,
And Skye feels the weight of a fate close at hand.
As the truth is revealed in a moment so bright,
The guest is the prince, bathed in soft light.

A cave or a castle it matters not—Juniper stands tall, a
timeless spot.

"Oh, Red Fox, why hide your true name?"
Sage asks in awe, her heart set aflame.
"Because would you have trusted my humble disguise?
I seek your hand, fair princess, beneath these skies."

Ask and you shall receive; the Juniper tree dares not
deceive.

With a gasp of delight, she knows what to say,
"Together we'll dance as the stars light our way."
A union of hearts, a celebration in song,
As Lark's sweet notes carry them all along.

Wisdom can often be seen in the essence and the roots of the
Juniper tree.

Thus Sage, Lark, and Skye, in harmony blend,
In a tale of enchantment that never shall end.
With joy in the air, their spirits take flight,
In the magic of Autumn, beneath the soft night.

Ekphrasis 7:

Ocher Reverie

HEY
chay
Ekphrasis 8:
Rushing Waves of
Sapphire

Vignette 5

Mid-Life Reflections

Autumn's Gumbo

It's a special occasion for my darling and I (me?)

The perfect time to make pumpkin, apple, and pecan pie (hot tea)

Don't forget the rosemary and thyme

Perfect undertones, rich flavors and smells to unwind

Garlic is a must, bell pepper, and ground sassafras leaves

Cloves, green onions, and scallions if you please

Pinch of spice makes everything taste just right

Cayenne pepper, to be precise

A roux for two, a deep earthy brew

Filled with Cajun spices, multiple meats and seafood

It's the perfect time to sit in front of a roaring fire

A book in one hand and in the other, hot apple cider

Watching the gumbo boil, the aromas almost too much to take

The added sweetness of pies as they bake

Makes my heart race

Itching for just a little taste

It's the perfect time to watch your precious face

Delighted by the smells, savoring every taste

Not knowing this is all a ploy, a plot to bring it all to a close

My love, desire for you, only the good Lord knows

It's the perfect time for the goodbyes to begin

I watched you pack your bags last night, my lover, my

sweetheart, my best friend

I know you're planning on skipping out

Not wanting to cry, fuss, or shout

Certainly not wanting to watch me pout

It's the perfect time, there's not a single doubt

My heart aches

My body shakes

I know this almost the end

But just a moment longer, can't we just pretend

That this is the perfect time to sit and unwind

To tell stories and reminisce one last time

To enjoy the tastes, sounds, and smells of the season

To enjoy Autumn's Gumbo, we don't need a reason.

As I Cry

As I cry, I have flashbacks of the not-so-distant past
Moments when I would come to you and reverence in your embrace
Every day I cry a little less and laugh a little more

I remember to count my many blessings, to cast my cares upon the shore
Into the sea of forgetfulness, I toss in the pain and the hurt
Into my prayer closet is where I shall return

As I cry, I remember to also pray
As I cry, I remember to also praise
As I cry, I remember to also worship

As I cry, I remember
I remember the craziness that was our life
The ups and downs, the ins and outs

I remember the lessons learned, the plans we made, the lashes I earned
I remember the fights we had, the talks and discussions shared, the strikes declared
I remember the family outings, the school plays, the affection and public displays

I remember, as I cry
As I cry, I cry a little less as time goes by
I have moments of doubt, of mistrust, of total disbelief

As I cry, I do so with more of a shout
A scream as though where you are you can hear the anger in my voice

How I miss you terribly, how I wish we could have
avoided this tragedy

As I cry, I wonder if I am selfish
If all of this is for nothing, because you are happier where
you are and well, I'm not
As I cry, I am thankful I got to say goodbye

We sang your favorite song,
Read your favorite psalm,
Prayed and then you were gone

As I cry, I continue to say goodbye,
Because I will never really concede
To believe that you are not here with me

As I cry
And I cry,
And I cry

I remember, I laugh, I shout
I sing, I dance, I pout
I reminisce, I reverence, I give thanks

As I cry, I cry for me more than I do for you
Because you are gone to heaven and I
I am stuck here lost without you

Run Free

The left hand cradles earth's deep breath,
the right holds the pulse of the endless sky —
fingers trace the storm's sharp edge,
cracks of light spill in every direction.

Time stretches, unwinds —
three thousand lifetimes in a moment,
as petals fall into one's grasp,
a sword twirls in the other,
sharp against the dance of wind.

Snow settles between the brows of mountains,
a quiet tear weeps through centuries —
this is me,
a fleeting sigh against the winds of change.

Left hand plucks the strings of fate,
the right dips a boat into the river's flow,
a red lotus blooms from the depths,
where troubles twist into something new.

Do not stop, do not waver,
point to the moon with trembling hands —
red lines of desire,
love spun in the silence between stars.

The left turns to feathers, soft and wild,
the right to scales, glimmering in the moonlight.
One life above the clouds,
another woven in the whispers of the forest,
dust on the breeze,
following through all worlds.

I gather it in my hands,
hold, release—
a dance of giving and taking,
until we are one,
two palms pressed together,
and the universe finds its place inside the heart.

Dreams Untold

The hands drift apart,
fingers brushing the edges of silence,
the earth cradled by one,
the sky carried by the other.
A space grows,
soft as twilight's edge,
where the winds whisper of untold journeys.

Years unspool like ancient threads,
woven into the fabric of the unseen,
each step a story
too quiet to speak,
yet loud as thunder in the soul's core.

The moon's glow fades,
and time folds itself away,
like petals dropped in a still stream —
we are everything and nothing at once,
caught between the spaces,
between the breaths of the earth and sky.

With every tear, a universe trembles,
every laugh, a world shifts —
and though the palms may part,
the heart holds a steady beat,
tender and unbroken.

We are dust,
we are flame,
we are the wind in the leaves —
and though dreams are untold,
they linger in the quiet

where time is not measured,
where love is not given or taken —
but simply known.

Journey to Nowhere

Each morning, the sun stretches its fingers
into the sky, soft as the turn of a page,
and I rise —
grateful for the gift,
for the words that fall like Autumn leaves,
gathering in the spaces between souls.

There is no doubt in the quiet hum,
no hesitation in the flight of thoughts —
just the pure joy of connection,
threads woven from heart to heart,
stories untold finally taking shape.

In the glow of this moment,
eyes meet eyes,
and something shifts —
not in the work,
but in the knowing,
the deep exhale of being seen,
of being heard at last.

A story carried on the wind,
twisting through branches,
it finds its place —
not to be judged,
but to be felt,
a spark that catches fire
in the silence between words.

This is where fulfillment blooms,
in the space where hearts beat
together —

where dreams are not distant stars,
but the rhythm of the earth beneath our feet.
A symphony of connection,
growing, endless,
as fleeting as the Autumn light.

I build with hands that do not divide
but weave into something whole,
something that holds us close
as we dance through this world
with the wind at our backs.

And still, each day, I wake,
and the sky whispers —
this journey is not a path,
but a gift,
a journey to nowhere,
and everywhere at once.

Shades of Gray

Shades of gray aren't really shades at all. Instead, they are the once vibrant colors that Autumn presented, boasted even, for our benefit. Purples and plums, fun for everyone. Blues and greens, for those blemishes unseen. Roses are red, violets are blue, shreds of dumplings entering a room, dancing and singing, a merry-go-round, the tides are turning, the ground slowly turning brown. Oranges and marmalade, cinnamon and spice, sugar and Stevia, wouldn't think twice.

Shades of gray, simply remind me of you. Where we are now, what we used to do. Falling leaves, dancing trees, singing birds, shifting world. Sands of time, grapes turned into wine, Autumn's love will always be mine. Shades of gray, aren't really shades of all. Instead, it is a timetable, of spring, summer, winter, and yes even fall.

Tears, Swing Low

Drip drop around the clock, I lay my face upon my pillow imagining your sweet embrace I will no longer be able to feel

Tick tock, where did the time go, some days feeling as though we are moving slow, others standing still, and yet a marathon now that you are gone.

I cry because I miss you, I cry because I cannot imagine this life without you, I cry because I cherish you, I cry because I never got the chance to say goodbye.

I smile because of what you mean to me, the memories I will forever hold near to my heart, sharing them with my children, my children's children, those near and those far.

I smile because of the laughter we shared, found memories of you doing my hair, great times of us debating political crimes, and yet

rewind, stop, pause, I learned more from you than I have from any class ever taught, and for that I thank you.

I smile because yours was infectious, you could light up an entire room, or tear it down with one smack down of your frown.

One look, and they were through, they knew not to play with you.

Fearless and ferocious, you were still faithful, righteous, and just. Ding dong, the doorbell played our song, never to be heard again,

I just can't bear to imagine that.

I close my eyes and dream a dream, and you are still here
with me.

I don't want to awake, no Lord, I can no longer take the
heartache

I dare not say goodbye.

With tears in my eyes, every drop is a prayer for you, from
my heart to our God in heaven,

May I always remember, never forget, the moments spent,
and the love shared,

The knowledge gained and the wisdom displayed, the
faithfulness grown, the seed of grace sown,

The epic nature song sung, swing low, sweet chariot,
coming to take me home
me home.

Herbs and Spice

Apple's warmth, a crisp whisper,
its skin wrapped in Autumn's embrace,
slicing through the silence —
a soft crunch, the earth's gift.

Orange, peeled like morning's first light,
segments unfold like dreams waiting —
sunshine trapped in each drop,
awakening the senses.

Basil, purple and sweet,
tangles with sage,
garden's breath and wild fennel,
woven into the wind's song.
Rosemary whispers secrets,
peppermint and spearmint —
cool as evening's kiss on the skin.

Lemongrass sways with the breeze,
its fresh green scent,
sharp as the last chill before nightfall.
Lavender hums in the distance,
a memory of fields,
ground cinnamon dusts the air —
a quiet warmth to the chill.

Together they blend,
in a quiet dance,
earth and sky,
herbs, fruits,
the pulse of a season's song.

Ice, like the first frost on morning's edge,
melts into the mix —
cool, yet soft as the falling leaves.
Water, coconut, a splash of clarity,
like dew on the dawn.

It's more than a sip,
more than a taste —
it's Autumn distilled,
captured in the breath of every leaf,
and every moment that sways
between the heat of summer
and the quiet of winter's coming.

Herbs and spice,
the essence of change —
a journey through the seasons,
from the orchard to the wild,
from the earth to the soul.

Blood Orange

Cayenne flickers,
its fire in the cool air —
a sharp sting to the tongue,
awakening the dusk of Autumn's breath.
Crushed chirata,
roots hidden deep in the earth,
whispers of ancient cures,
leaves flutter like distant memories.

Lemongrass, crushed,
its citrus dances with the wind,
lifting the heaviness from the world,
its tang sharp like the bite of the season.
Lemon peel curls,
a yellowed ghost of summer's warmth,
its bitter sweetness held by time.

Sage, crushed, crumbles like old thoughts,
soaked in silence,
grounded in the soil of understanding.
Lavender, small and fragile,
but with a scent that lingers in the fading light,
a sigh before the frost.

Tarragon — green veins of the forest,
its memory tied to the earth's slow rhythm,
as the days shrink and the nights stretch long.
Each leaf a story,
each spice a thread in the tapestry,
woven from the harvest's whispers.

In the bowl, they come together,

fragments of summer's fading heat,
wrapped in Autumn's embrace.
The blend settles,
stored in the cool, darkened places —
like the quiet before the first snow.

A pinch on the tongue —
heat, brightness,
an echo of fire and frost,
Autumn held in the breath of an orange,
the season suspended,
waiting for the winds to shift.

Blood orange,
the pulse of change,
as it stirs in the depths,
a flavor that lingers long after
the leaves have fallen.

When Day Meets Night

Jasmine, a breath of morning mist, suspended between the earth's warmth
and the cool kiss of dusk— it unfurls in quiet anticipation,
a promise, soft and light.

Ginger pulses like the heart of the fading sun, its heat slow-burning,
mingling with the chill of twilight, where shadows stretch long,
and time is a flicker, a flash between the fading gold and rising silver.

Hibiscus, red like the last bloom of summer, cradles the warmth of the day in its petals,
pressed gently into the evening air. A scarlet echo of life that will soon fold into the night.

Hemp hearts, soft and grounding, fall into the night's embrace,
anchored in the quiet hum of the earth, while chia seeds scattered like stardust,
blurring the edges of space and time, a pulse between moments.

Lemongrass, fresh with the dawn, enters the coolness of evening
as the day fades away— its citrus tang, a breath of the wind rising with the moon.

Peppermint, sharp and crisp, is the cool whisper in the night air,
a spark of clarity in the dark that pushes the weight of shadows away with its clean bite.

Wild cherry, a flicker of sweetness, the last warmth before
the chill
of fall claims the air, while angelica root, deep and old,
whispers forgotten secrets beneath the soil, as time turns
on.

Elderberries, black as night, tangle with passion flowers,
opening like dreams that stretch into the void — an offering
to the stars.

Alfalfa, nettle, thistle, roots tangled with the earth's pulse,
drawing from its deep breath before the frost comes.
Dandelion, fierce in its resilience, holds the remnants of
summer's warmth,
fighting the coolness with every breath.

Cardamom, tiny seeds of fire, ignite the heart,
flaring briefly before retreating into the night's cool arms.

Wild hearts, elderberries and damiana, lavender and
raspberry, whisper secrets to the moon,
drifting between the last rays of the setting sun and the first
breath of night.
A wild scent carried on the wind, as memory stirs with the
turning of the seasons.

A steeped blend, a sip of what lingers — the delicate
balance between
day's end and night's beginning, where warmth and chill
meet in the silence,
and the world pauses — if only for a moment.

All Is Not Lost

A storm of berries ripples through the air,
picking up pieces of summer's final warmth —
antioxidants unfurling like soft wings,
lifting the weight of time,
fighting the fatigue of seasons past,
mending the wear and tear with every bite.

Chia seeds and flax gather at the edges,
tiny gifts of earth,
woven fibers that guide the rhythm of breath,
smoothing the journey through the body's maze,
tuning the heart to a steady hum,
whispering promises of balance.

Nuts, glistening in their earthy sheen,
hold the pulse of the earth in their flesh,
silken oils cradling the heart,
keeping it warm,
guarded —
the bitter winds of winter cannot touch
what is protected by their embrace.

Damiana and lavender,
wild petals unfurling beneath the twilight,
murmur of peace
in the crackling air —
they settle the restless mind,
easing the pull of stress,
until the edges of the day soften
like the last rays of a fading sun.

In every drop of fruit,
there is a wellspring of hydration,
feeding the spirit with cool clarity —
a promise that nothing is lost,
not in the turning of the world,
not in the shifting of seasons,
for the earth, the body,
and the heart know
how to heal,
how to renew,
how to be whole.

Autumn's Memory

Leaves tremble, as though reaching
To the edges of an unwritten sky
A dance caught in the slow turning of time,
Where each moment sways on the breeze,
An eternal waltz between earth and sky.

Herbs of gold and fire,
Cayenne and sage,
Clash in the cool air,
Their whispers stitch the fabric of season,
Their warmth rising from the earth
Like a secret meant only for the knowing.

Berries ripen beneath the ache of a waning sun,
Shining with the last light,
The earth's heart beating beneath the frost.
From the bones of this land,
A pulse of vitality hums,
Its breath carried in the winds of change.

Hibiscus and elderberries,
Passion flowers tracing the arc of the sky,
Remind us of that quiet truth
Autumn is a gathering,
A collection of moments,
Each one a piece of memory
Falling like golden leaves into the wind.
Fennel and rosemary,
Lemongrass,
Smoke of lavender rising
Where once the fire burned bright.

Through fields of thyme and tarragon,
Memories stretch out
Boundless, unbroken
Woven between the rustling leaves

And the shadow of every setting sun.
The scent of jasmine lingers on the air,
A perfume of the wild heart,
Alive in every breath.

Sage crumbles beneath fingers
As the last light leaves the day,
Suspended in the mist of evening.
It is the knowing, the steady touch of time
The pull of the moon against the stillness,
Where the earth and sky meet
In a dance that lasts forever.

We are lost, we are found,
Woven into the tapestry of this hour,
Drawn into the colors of this season
Purple basil and fennel fronds,
The sweetness of tarragon,
And the heat of cayenne,
Gripping us like a long-forgotten memory
Caught between summer's end
And the silence of winter's approach.

The winds carry with them
The laughter of those we've lost,
The ones who whispered secrets to the trees,
The ones who danced through the fields
Underneath the very same stars.
Now their words echo
In the silence of the fall air,
Lilting and soft,
As though they never left.

We listen, we remember,
We breathe in the cool, crisp air
The scent of thyme and wild berries,
The crackle of frost gathering on the edge of dusk.
Every bite of this moment,
A taste of something long ago,

Now made whole again in the space between
The last light of Autumn
And the quiet of winter's breath.

Autumn's memory swirls,
Catching fragments of time
We are here,
We are lost,
We are found again,
Woven into the threads of a world that spins,
Ever turning, ever waiting,
For the return of all we've forgotten.

Each leaf that falls,
Each herb that bends in the cold,
Is a reminder:
Autumn does not die.
It lingers in the spaces between
The turning of days,
In the scent of lavender,
In the pulse of the earth beneath our feet,
Holding us,
Waiting for us to remember,
That we have always been here.

Ekphrasis 9:

Ethereal Twilight

Hey chay
Ekphrasis 9:
Ethereal Twilight

Ekphrasis 10:

Liquid Poetry of Autumn

Ekphrasis 10:
Liquid Poetry of
Autumn

Vignette 6

The Final Thoughts

Autumn's Garden

In the hush between dawn and dusk,
the garden breathes a soft sigh,
where the last of summer clings to its fading warmth —
a quiet dance, a fading song.
Here, in the cool whisper of the breeze,
basil's fragrance rises from the earth,
interwoven with the crisp scent of fallen leaves,
the memory of the sun still trapped in their veins.

Lavender nods to the sky,
a quiet gesture, a whispered secret.
Peppermint curls like tendrils of smoke,
spiraling into the corners of the air,
where rosemary waits, steadfast,
its green hands reaching toward the heavens.
Each herb carries the taste of time —
of sun-drenched mornings and moonlit nights.

Beneath the shifting shadows of branches,
elderberries dot the landscape,
black pearls clinging to the vine,
while tarragon and thyme hum in soft refrain,
their voices barely a murmur
beneath the weight of Autumn's quiet arrival.
Chia seeds glisten, hidden beneath a blanket of leaves,
their tiny promises waiting to awaken.

In this garden, time feels both endless and fleeting,
where the air is thick with the earth's gentle ache,
and the sound of dry leaves crunching beneath
is the music of memories,
unraveled and re-woven with each passing wind.

Hibiscus blooms, a burst of warmth against the cold,
its petals unfurling like stories half-told,
waiting for the touch of frost to turn them to song.

The winds carry with them the last whispers of summer,
but Autumn presses its hand upon the world —
silent, steady, and true.
Each petal, each leaf, each grain of soil
is both a departure and a beginning,
for here in the fading light,
we are caught between the old and the new,
the memory of warmth and the promise of winter.

This garden holds us gently,
its roots tangled in our veins,
its scent woven into the very air we breathe,
reminding us that in the quiet of Autumn's embrace,
there is both a letting go and a return —
a cycle that moves beyond seasons,
and into the timeless heart of all things.

As My Tears Fall

Seasons change and the gazelle appears in the moonlight so clear. Gently saunter, elegant and luxurious, the dapper haltingly appears amongst the thorns and bushes of the garden patches filled with lilies and lilacs. The sweet aroma fills the air as their eyes meet in concert with the musical sounds provided by the birds, crickets, and amazingly soulful creatures of the forest. The heart wants what the heart desires above all. As my tears fall.

Welcome savory Autumn, welcome back to my sanctuary, fill me with your wise words and the tenderness of your warm touch. You've grown on me, my precious friend, with your refined palate and stylish virility. Do you still remember that tender moment when our hearts encountered each other, oh how our minds and souls were soon in succession. Seasons change, nevertheless, the heart craves what the heart is desperate for. As my tears fall.

A ballad for you my dear heart. A psalm that speaks a language only our hearts can translate and understand. I reach out to you, but where is your hand? I cry out for you in a way only you can comprehend. I sing this song to you. Seasons change. The sun rises and sets. The moon, never before so undaunted and stunning in its embodiment in the night skyline. Seasons change, but time ever stays still, for the heart longs for what the heart yearns for. As my tears fall.

A stream flowing into a lake, floating into a river, falling into an ocean. So are the depths of despair and audacious attempts to love a transient, yet extraordinarily exquisite soul as yours. Seasons change, yet I remain, ever diligent undiminished in my conviction that loving you is what I was born and built to do. As my tears fall.

An impassioned outcry for your attention reflective of my affections is unattainable. I gather the tears that have fallen from season to season to create this stunning ocean view for you. The Waterfalls of Ambrose Elio. named for you, my "immortal sun." For it is the love capitulated in my tears that pours out for only you. Shine bright. As the fire reduces to smoke, this flame shall never be extinguished, neither shall my love.

Echoes of Cheraw

I see you wrestling with the wind
Always running, fighting, never wanting to bend
Riverbanks follow your lead, never wavering, ever so
steadily
Your trusty stallion standing tall beside you

Dancing with the foliage, singing to the trees
Cherishing every moment spent with me
Reds and yellows, greens and purples, all captivated and
cultivated in mother earth
The Carolinas never knew how much it was worth

Cabbage and corn, peppers and onions, all pleasant to the
senses of man
Everything under the sun, grown by the Cheraw's hand
I remember you my tender-hearted friend
I recall your very last stand

I saw you with my own eyes reach out your hand
A sign of hope, love, and generosity to those arriving on a
strange land
Your kindness did not go unnoticed, your memories
forever will be preserved
The love and mercy you showed to others, inspired your
names forever seen in the clouds above

Your voices of song and cheer
Whispers through the waves of the wind in every ear
Your sacrifice forever and always will never be forgotten
Every day, sunrise to sunset, tilling the earth, sweet
potatoes, rainbow corn, squash, and cotton

How you stood for love, peace, grace, and pride

Your faith seen clearly in every step of your stride
Your legacy continues to stand the test of time
The values you lived by and passed down through verse
and rhyme

Your family, your heritage, your people continue to stand
Fighting against oppression any who dared to shackle the
human hand
It was clear from day one you and your kind were the
chosen ones
Your legacy for generations, the stories of the first nations

We remember and we share with all far and wide
How you loved, how you lived, and how you died
We thank you for your teachings and your prayers too
May The Echoes of the Cheraw continually be heard and
felt in the souls, hearts, and minds of all who cherish you

The Memory of You

The memory of you. A welcomed torture to my soul. A profound revelation, reminder of our final destination. Tomorrow. Tomorrow. Tomorrow is not promised. Elegance, a smell only exuded by the essence of Autumn's most exuberant hues of gold, orange, and burgundy. Ambiance, enriched by the senses, winds shifting and blowing, echoing my loneliness that only can be exasperated by the utter hopeless despair in endless whispers of farewell as the season departs, makes way for my cold dark heart, taken over by fraternal art, overwhelmed by maternal arches, undertaken by dwindling views and fading blues. All that is left to get me through. The memory of you.

Flickering Light

The pulse of the earth hums beneath the frost,
deep roots stirred by the waning light.
Autumn bends the trees,
whispering the language of the soil.

In the stillness, time slows to a murmur,
each leaf a memory pressed into the soil,
carrying the weight of harvest,
the fleeting echo of seasons passed.

The wind breathes low, like a quiet chant,
stirring the earth's bones,
fingers of warmth dissolving
into the cool hands of evening.

Beneath the blanket of a fading sky,
the earth, alive with the pulse of change,
offers its final breath —
an offering of amber and ash,
before the darkness swallows the horizon whole.

In this flickering light, we are shadows,
rooted in the soil,
becoming one with the whisper of winds,
the rhythm of the earth,
its song forever unbroken.

Last of the Wild

The earth hums beneath the steep hills, where basalt and
wind are one,
and the scent of tangerine peel clings to the cool air —
a fragrance that dances with the salt of the sea.

Golden leaves, soft as whispers, flutter from the gnarled
branches of the camellias.
The sun dips low, spilling its light like amber over the
fields, casting long shadows that thread through the
emerald vines. Here, the wild things remember.

In the wind, the songs of crickets pulse, faint and fleeting,
murmuring their farewell to the stillness that settles over
the island.
The waves crash on blackened rocks, their rhythm steady,
unwavering,
like the heartbeat of the land itself.

Through the scent of pine and damp moss, an old song
echoes —
of wind-scarred shores and sky that carries memories,
a song that swells with the ripening fruit, the last of the
wild.

Beneath the clouds, a glimpse of the ancient Hallasan, its
breath heavy with fog,
as the mountain watches over the land, steady in its eternal
pulse.
A scent of earth and sea and stone, woven into the last
harvest of Autumn.

In this stillness, we remember the pulse that thrums
beneath our feet,

the wildness of the island fading softly into the fading twilight.

The earth sighs, quieted by the season's embrace, and the last of the wild holds its breath.

Farewell Fading Daylight

A wave farewell doesn't seem right
A scream and a shout goodbye just aren't polite
A party to say adiós simply won't do
A brunch and matinee to leave you
Well that's just not enough
In love and honor, depart we must
Farewell fading daylight, I'll simply say
Until we meet again, do svidaniya, as I walk away

Ashes of Greed

From the carbon in ashes, you are reborn,

Worn around the neck, ears, fingers, or the wrist as a good

luck charm.

How could this be,

The process of turning pain into property?

Life was never meant to be repurposed this way,

To be recreated, transposed, and put on display.

Ashes to ashes, dust to dust is what every priest under the

sun used to say.

Now instead, death has been traded for a payday.

How could life and death be treated this way?

Where's the love, compassion, respect?

Was it traded for fame, fortune, whatever you could get?

I tell you what I know is true:

If you could sell the human soul, you'd do that too.

The greed of mankind never ceases to amaze.

This is a sad generation, neglectful, disrespectful,

intellectually and spiritually unfazed.

Death will not remain silent; it will come one day for you

too.

Diamonds may live forever, but this won't be true for you.

Reduced to a single insignificant piece of glass,

The indecency of it all — tragedy, lack of class.

Mark my words, regret is a fickle mistress,

One that collects and never misses.

You have been forewarned, and truth be told,

No piece of jewelry could ever capture the human soul.

The White Silhouette

Autumn came early this year with cool breezes whispering in my ear. Singing softly a lover's ballad so gentle, so sweet, over and over again on repeat. Sunsets and orange marmalade, country crock butter on toast, soup filled days. Redtop country house glowing in the horizon, marvelous bay windows with a central view of an old tire swing. Closer to the end I see faintly drifting between the leaves, dangling and dancing amongst the willow trees.

The white silhouette is everything to me, all that I ever thought of, all I ever dreamt to be. So free and fair, not a care to bare, music no one else could hear but me as I drift off into the eternal glare. Silver and marble know no end, giant yet subtle footsteps lead me in.

Rainbow glows and golden hue's, glistening teardrops shaped as diamonds. A quick spin and all I could see- through rose-colored glasses was the white silhouette with clear precision. Dawned with touches of opal and sapphire, rubies and pearls, all I could envision.

Bronze feet, fire for eyes, wool for hair, and hands of cotton. Baritone voice echoes through the willows, rising far above the clouds, clear beyond the seas. Appearing to ride on angel's wings, is this but a dream? The white silhouette comes closer to me, beckoning my name, crying for me. Yet, I do not fear, I'm not afraid, closer I go as in a daze.

The white silhouette is in front of me, clear as day in all its glory. Holding my hand, he leads me in, well done my child, he says to me. I know it wasn't easy but you made it through, I know you had questions but your doubts never grew. I know you had troubles but you triumphed in the end.

Well done my child, I'm so proud of you. Your faith has carried you over, your love has brought you through. In my house, there is room for you. No more suffering or pain or tears from you. Your reward is waiting as I've always promised to provide. Welcome back my child I'm so proud of you, welcome home once again, right by my side.

Epilogue: The Endless Cycle

Through my eyes, you've witnessed Autumn's journey unfold—a journey filled with growth, challenges, and lessons learned. Yet, many of the figures who played a role in shaping this path have not been named this time. Their stories, woven intricately into the fabric of Autumn's tale, remain for another time. Along the way, Autumn crossed paths with many others—figures who stirred the air, shifting the course of events. Some brought chaos, while others brought clarity; some ignited tension, while others sparked moments of joy. Each one, though different, contributed to the tapestry of Autumn's life, teaching valuable lessons about the world and the self.

There were those who challenged Autumn's beliefs, urging a confrontation with fears and doubts, and those who showed the beauty of self-discovery, reminding that change is not something to fear but something to embrace. Others still taught resilience, the strength found not in avoiding struggle but in rising from it time and time again. And there were those who reminded Autumn of the importance of connection, of community, and of the relationships that shape us through the seasons of life.

But not all of these figures have been revealed yet. Their stories are waiting, just beyond the horizon. Some are wrapped in mystery, others in complexity, and each will have their part to play in Autumn's continuing journey. Their influence, subtle or profound, will guide as Autumn moves forward, learning, growing, and evolving with every twist of fate.

I have watched it all. From above, I have seen Autumn's story unfold, silent but constant, a witness to the beauty and struggles of this path. And as the embodiment of time itself, I carry the wisdom of the seasons — the wisdom of change. This journey, this story, is far from over.

Autumn's Ballad is more than a melody — it is a symphony, and the notes are still being written. The winds will continue to whisper, the leaves will continue to fall, and the cycle will carry on. There are still many changes to come, many lessons to learn, and many stories left to be told.

So, as you close this chapter, know that the road ahead is still unfolding. You have only just begun to hear the song, and its true harmony is yet to reveal itself. Let me be your guide once more as we embark on the next phase of Autumn's journey, where new figures will emerge, and the symphony will grow ever more complex, ever more beautiful.

Acknowledgments

I would like to extend my deepest gratitude to the remarkable individuals who have shaped my journey and made this book possible.

To my loving departed mother Ellender and my amazing father John, thank you for your unwavering love and support. Your guidance has been the foundation of my dreams, and I am forever grateful for the values you instilled in me.

To my children, Geneva and Johnathan, your laughter and joy inspire me every day. You are my greatest treasures, and I hope this work reflects the love and lessons I strive to share with you. To my bonus babies Samaya, Samuel II, Nathanial, Kayla, Quincy, KiKi, and Valentina and Valeria, being part of your lives has been a true blessing. You are all gifts I never anticipated, but I wholeheartedly welcomed and cherish each of with all my heart. Thank you for allowing me to share in your journey; you have enriched my life in ways I can't express.

To my best friend Amy, thank you for your unwavering support and companionship. Your presence in my life is a gift, and your encouragement has motivated me through every challenge. I love you, sister!

To my mentors, your wisdom and encouragement have been invaluable. Thank you for believing in me and for sharing your insights, which have fueled my passion and creativity.

To Dr. R. L. Robertson, Sr., thank you for your guiding hand. You have been a port in the storm, an unexpected blessing. Your wisdom, guidance, and support are something that I am profoundly grateful for. I thank God for placing you in my life.

To my cousins Sherrel Gail, Cynthia, Pam, Lisa, Monica, Stacy, Shakesia, Shemika, Liza, and Aldricka, you have been my rock; the support you've given means the world to me. Thank you for the laughter, the memories, and the bonds we share. You have brought joy and strength to my life, and I am grateful for each moment we've spent together.

To my inner circle, Obossey, Regan, Stephanie, Kim, Danny, Donna Kay, Oneisha, Ashia, Jeanne, Carolyn, Paul, and Miracle, your prayers, testimonies, love, care, kindness, and tenderness have carried me through some of the toughest and darkest times in my life. Because of your unwavering support, I was able to see the light, feel the wind on my face, and embrace the possibilities that awaited me on the other side. I am endlessly grateful for each of you.

This book is a celebration of all of you. Your love and support have made this journey not just possible, but truly meaningful. Thank you. I love you all! ~C

About the Author

Experience the Effusiveness, Embrace the Essence, and Enjoy the Exhilaration of Autumn's Ballad with C. L. Pinto Martinez.

Chandra L. Pinto Martinez, writing under the pen name C. L. Pinto Martinez, is a whirlwind of talent and creativity, embodying countless roles: graphic designer, marketer, lecturer, instructor, business owner, radio host, podcaster, writer, poet, and lyricist—the list goes on! Yet, above all these impressive titles, the ones that truly resonate with her heart are mother, daughter, sister, aunt, friend, and beloved child of God.

Hailing from the vibrant Cajun country, C. L. proudly claims Baton Rouge, Louisiana, as her home. Her adventurous spirit has led her to live in five different states and explore many more, earning her the delightful title of nomad. A passionate writer since the age of 12, C. L. has seen her poetry grace the pages of numerous publications, alongside her academic and professional works in various mediums. Each word she crafts reflects her rich experiences and deep connections, inviting others to join her on this beautiful journey of life.

The novelette in verse unfolds as a heartfelt love song between the author and Autumn. Through these lyrical pages, the human experience is vividly visualized and beautifully vocalized, capturing our profound connection to nature. It explores the challenges, trials, triumphs, struggles, victories, realizations, revelations, and reconciliations of the human heart as it navigates its own internal battles. Each stanza invites readers to journey alongside the author, celebrating both the beauty and complexity of life intertwined with the enchanting essence of Autumn.

Faith and family are the cornerstones of C. L.'s life. When she's not busy creating a better world with her loved ones, she can often be found waterfall hunting in the picturesque hills and mountains of the Carolinas, especially during the enchanting season of Autumn. *Autumn's Ballad* marks her debut book, a heartfelt expression of her love for both nature and the human experience.

For interviews, speaking engagements, review copies, collaborations, or additional information regarding this work, please reach out to the contacts below. We welcome all media, literary, and professional inquiries and are happy to assist with your request.

Primary Media Contact

House of Chay (Imprint of Hey Chay Press)
Contact: C. L. Pinto Martinez
Phone: (843) 420-9757
Email:
hello@officialheychay.com
Social Media: @officialheychay
Website: www.heychay.com

Scan to Learn More

Publisher Contact

Hadassah's Crown Publishing, LLC
634 NE Main Street #1263
Simpsonville, SC 29681
Phone: (864) 708-1214
Email:hadassahscrown@gmail.com
Social Media: @hadassahscrownpublishing
Website:
https://www.hadassahscrownpublishing.com

Scan to Learn More